#THEBOYFRIENDDARE

BOOK 4 OF THE #BESTFRIENDSFOREVER SERIES

YESENIA VARGAS

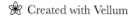 Created with Vellum

For my dear sister, Ana, and all her awesome support. And for my daughters.

ONE

You know that one boy in high school? Short and kind of chubby? Could still pass for a seventh grader?

Everyone leaves for summer break at the end of sophomore year, and he waves goodbye.

Then you bump into him on the first day of school, and you don't even recognize him?

All of a sudden, he's six feet tall, sporting facial hair, and you can SEE his muscles through his t-shirt?

That was Ian.

He was practically my best friend, especially during soccer season.

And the first day of junior year, I'd been the one to bump into him and practically spit out my iced coffee because I couldn't believe how ridiculously handsome he'd become in the last three months.

Amazing what a summer of sleeping in and working out could do for a guy.

Of course, the girls at school had immediately noticed him, couldn't get enough of him. I still wasn't sure how he'd remained single all of last year.

But as hot as he suddenly was, the two of us had stayed friends. I wasn't sure I could ever see him as more than that. Maybe that image of the short and chubby version of him was too ingrained into my mind.

Or maybe I'd never risk the awesome, one-of-a-kind friendship we had. It just wasn't worth it.

In any other case, I'd be the first one in my group of best friends to kiss a cute guy just for the fun of it, but even I drew a line when it came to Ian.

So when soccer season rolled around during senior year, he was still one of my closest friends.

We sat together on the bus ride home from the first away soccer game of the season.

This was my favorite time of year because it meant varsity boys and girls soccer games every Friday night. Then eating out after and having a great time, no matter if we won or lost.

But if we won, there was some guaranteed craziness to be had, usually instigated by me with a hesitant Ian watching nearby.

That was the case tonight.

We'd creamed our opponents tonight, totally mopped the floor with them, and it felt awesome.

Nothing like the high of victory, your muscles still warm, sweat soaking your jersey.

I joined the screaming guys and girls on the bus

and began my favorite chant. Y-E-L-L, Y-E-L-L, EVERYBODY YELL. GO WESTWOOD, YEAH, YEAH, GO WESTWOOD!

When everyone was nice and loud and Coach covered his ears with his clipboard, I knew my work was done.

With a wide grin, I sat down and turned to Ian.

He shook his head and stuck his earbuds in. "You love getting them all riled up," he said.

I took that as a compliment. "Why, thank you."

I scooted forward so my knees rested on the seat in front of me.

Ian took his earbuds back out. "I do have to say, though, those two goals you shot tonight were pretty impressive. Especially the one during the last five minutes of the game. You had the entire boys team going wild. I'm pretty sure Chris actually peed his pants."

I burst out laughing. "What about you? Were you going wild?"

Ian scoffed. "Are you kidding me? I was just trying to make sure no one got a concussion or something."

It had been a pretty good game. Definitely the best one so far. I couldn't wait to see what the rest of the season would hold. "You played pretty good yourself," I said. "You stopped how many goals? At least five?"

Ian was goalie this year since last year's goalie had graduated back in the spring. Plus with his six-foot plus stature, he had pretty much been a sure pick, even though the boys' coach had barely given him a second glance last year.

Ian had mostly sat on the bench then, hoping to get some game time in, but I was glad he was finally getting his moment to shine.

It was pretty evident he'd worked really hard over the summer.

He'd gone from second string to starting every single game, and he deserved it. The boys were on their way to an awesome season thanks to him.

I pulled out my phone and tapped the camera icon. Then I made a crazy face with my tongue out, leaning my head to the side so Ian was in view.

Just as I took the picture, he saw what I was doing and smiled. His perfect pearly whites, a huge difference from the braces he wore until freshman year, instantly made the picture Instagram-worthy. Not even counting his disheveled, dirty blonde hair and visible Adam's apple.

What was it about a guy's Adam's apple that drove me crazy? I had no idea.

I posted the picture and showed Ian. He grinned and gave me a thumbs up in approval. Then he offered me an earbud.

Ian loved music, and he had specific playlists he listened to before a game. I'd made the habit of listening with him since last year, and it'd really made a difference for me when I played. Plus he had really good taste in music.

After a few minutes, we zoned out to the beat of

the songs. Ian stared out the window into the evening sky, and I went through my Instagram notifications. My picture was already up to twenty likes, including the #BFFs.

Then my phone dinged with a text.

Tori: He's cute. Latest #forfunsies guy?

I shook my head and smiled.

Lena: No way. That's Ian.

Tori: THAT'S IAN? He looks different than I remember.

Harper: Agreed on the hotness.

Rey: ^

Ella: Very nice smile.

Tori: And hair…

Lena: What can I say? Growth spurt. Lol. But seriously, he did become pretty handsome. Just friends, though.

Another ding rang through my ears, but I realized it was Ian's phone.

I glanced at him, and he held up his phone, a crooked smile on his face. "Sorry. It's Bethany."

"Here," I said, giving him back his earbud. Then I scooted away just a tad.

Bethany was Ian's girlfriend as of two months ago. Pretty much since the first week of school. She'd been the one to successfully pounce on him and nab him, much to the disappointment of the entire girls' varsity soccer team.

Bethany was your typical high school babe. Long legs, long sleek blonde hair down past her shoulders. She always looked like she was on her way to a magazine photo shoot.

Most boys went crazy over her, but I secretly couldn't stand her. I held back eye rolls whenever she was around. She thought the world revolved around her. Plus she barely scraped by in school and didn't bother to do any extracurriculars. Probably for fear of breaking a nail.

I had no idea what Ian saw in her—probably just the outside—but he'd lost so many cool points when I found out they were an item.

I went back to the text messages on my phone.

Oh yeah. Just friends.

I tapped out another message.

Lena: Besides, he has a girlfriend, you guys. Bethany?

Ella sent a blank expression emoji while Tori sent a thumbs down. They weren't fans of Bethany either.

Rey: And what if he didn't have a girlfriend? Would you ever go for it?…

That was an interesting question.

I thought about it for a second, taking a quick look at Ian, who was busy texting Bethany.

There was so much more to him than his good looks. He was also a really great guy.

But no.

Lena: Nope. He's probably the one boy I'd never dare kiss.

Harper: Not even for funsies? ;)

Lena: Nuh uh. He's too good of a friend. Not sure I could even see him as anything more. It'd be weird.

Sure, I missed us talking like we used to, but that was it.

My friends and I started chatting about other

stuff, but as the bus rumbled on home through the night, I couldn't get my mind off of Rey's question.

If Bethany wasn't in the picture, would I ever go for it?

I exhaled. No, I reminded myself.

Definitely not.

Ian was just a friend.

TWO

By the time the bus pulled into Westwood High, our plans for the rest of the night were set.

Party at one of the boys' house in an hour.

Coach pretended not to listen to what we had in store for celebrating and reminded us of a job well done.

My dad was already waiting for me in his pickup in the parking lot. My parents had just gotten me a car of my own, but on game days, Dad still liked to drop me off at school, pick me up after my game, and ask me how things went on the way home.

After telling him the play-by-play, he nodded, and I knew that meant he thought I did great. That was his style.

Unlike me, he was a man of few words, and if he usually had to say something, it was to give me pointers or advice on how to get past defenders or how I should have taken a better shot.

He'd played and coached for most of his life, so it

was really thanks to him that I played soccer so well. He'd taught me from the time I could walk. Same with my older brothers and older sister. My brothers loved to play, my sister not really, but he said I was the one who could really go far if I stuck with it.

Most of my brothers had been decent or even good, but they hadn't stuck with it.

For me, though, soccer was everything.

It was the main reason I tolerated school and got good grades. So I could stay on the team.

Dribbling the ball at my feet, surrounded by bright green grass, the field a blur all around me, and the rapid rise and fall of my chest as I pushed my body to the max to outrun a defender and shoot... There wasn't anything else quite like it.

Except maybe kissing boys.

My dad didn't really know about that, though, so we kept our conversations around soccer.

We got home, and with a quick thanks to Dad, I ran into the house.

Within forty-five minutes, I was back out of my room. Showered. Hair blow-dried and straightened. Favorite outfit on. Eyeliner and lip gloss on point.

I found my parents in the living room. My older brothers had long ago moved out, and my sister was out with her friends. I had plans for my Friday night too.

Standing by the TV, I said, "Hey, is it okay if I go to a party for a couple hours?"

My dad turned his gaze from their usual Mexican soap to me. "*A donde y con quien?*" he asked in Spanish.

I said something about hanging out with the soccer team and parents being there, but I wasn't even sure about the second part.

He grunted in response, and I knew that meant yes. I shrieked and gave him a hug.

My mom didn't look so happy about it. "Text us when you get there, Lena. Don't forget. And make sure you're home by eleven," she chided.

I went in and gave her a peck on the cheek. "I won't forget. I'll text you guys when I get there and before I leave. Promise."

My parents used to make my brothers chaperone me when I was in middle school up until ninth grade. Then it was my older sister Maria, and we had to go everywhere together if we were allowed to do anything.

Now that she was in college and I was almost eighteen, my mom and dad seemed to be adapting to modern times and letting us girls go out alone and unsupervised. Not that my brothers ever had that problem.

#BeingLatina

Or maybe my newfound freedom was due to the fact that I was the youngest and my dad had always given me free reign compared to her. That's what Maria always said anyway.

Maria said a lot of things, though.

Within fifteen minutes, I was at the party. It was already in full swing, and I'd texted the #BFFs before leaving the house, inviting them to join us.

My phone buzzed as I walked in. But before I

could look at it, Chris and several of the varsity boys whooped and cheered when they saw me.

"Lena! You're our hero!" Chris said.

I gave them a dazzling smile and joined everybody in the living room. "Where's Ian?" I asked Perry.

"Not here yet," she replied.

I wondered if he'd bring Bethany along with him. She usually hung onto him like a barnacle or something.

Whipping my phone out of my back pocket, I finally checked my messages.

One from Ian. A couple new ones in the #BFFs thread.

I opened the message from Ian first.

Ian: Where are you?

Lena: Just got to the party. I thought you were coming?

I waited for a reply and chatted with some of the girls, but after a couple minutes, nothing.

Then I remembered to read my other messages.

Tori: Be there soon :)

Rey: Is it going to be all soccer people?

She sent a side-looking eye emoji after that.

Harper: Assuming it's okay if we bring bfs? :)

Lena: BFs welcome <3 and yes, mostly soccer people lol but it's going to be a lot of fun!

Half an hour later, the party was really going. Great music, dancing, and lots of laughing. Plus my mom would have been happy to know that Chris's mom popped in from time to time.

My friends walked through the door, but still no

Ian. Maybe he'd decided to hang out with Bethany alone, so I gave my full attention to my friends.

I tried giving them the play-by-play too, but it was way over their heads.

After trying to explain off-sides too many times, I gave up. "Basically, I made two goals, which was awesome," I said.

Rey stared blankly. "Only two? So four points?" she tried.

I giggled. "No, two goals. Two points total. In soccer, that's a big deal. I think you're thinking basket-ball, where each basket is worth two points."

Ella nodded. "That's what Jesse plays, remember?"

Tori made a motion like she was shooting a ball.

Rey frowned and continued staring blankly. "I don't get it," she said.

Harper leaned in toward her and whispered loudly. "Me neither. I pretend. Just nod along."

We laughed and got up to go get refills on our drinks.

I poured out orange soda for myself and passed the two-liter bottle around. Then Ian walked in, his hands in his jacket pockets.

"Ian," I said. "You came."

He looked off, his eyes downcast and his mouth in a frown. "Hey," he said. "I was wondering where you were."

My friends glanced back and forth between us, and I remembered to introduce them.

They gave Ian small waves or a smile, and Ian gave a half-hearted wave back.

Harper looked to the other girls and me. "Lena, we'll meet you back in the living room?" she asked.

I nodded. "Sure."

The girls left, leaving Ian and me alone in the kitchen. The music was still pretty loud in here, but we could talk normally. He joined me next to the counter.

I studied his face. His usual easy-going grin was missing. "You okay?"

He exhaled, and I'd never seen his eyes like that. Sad and kind of empty. It made my chest feel empty too. "Bethany broke up with me," he said quietly.

I gasped. "What? Why?" I demanded.

Ian shrugged, and my heart broke a little for him, just seeing how crushed he was. "She said I haven't been spending enough time with her with soccer going on, and maybe she wants to date this college guy anyway. Says she's over 'dumb high school relationships.'"

I scoffed, not believing she'd actually said all that stuff to Ian. "What a jerk," I cried. "She's already got her eyes on some other guy?" Of course Bethany would. I couldn't even say I was surprised. I put my hand on top of his. "Ian, you are way too good for her. You know that, right?"

He shrugged again, refusing to look anywhere but the white granite counter in front of him. "I really liked her, you know?" He sighed. "Still do." He finally met my eyes. "Am I a fool for saying that?"

I paused for a second, taking in the hurt on his face. Then I shook my head. "Not at all."

We didn't say anything, and I could tell that was about as much as he wanted to say about the whole thing, so I gave him a hug. He hardly hugged me back, but I knew not to take it personally.

This was the reason I preferred to kiss for funsies and not for realsies. The risk of heartbreak wasn't worth it. At least for me.

Bethany had been Ian's first real girlfriend, and she'd gone and stomped on it before kicking it into the trash can.

Part of me wished I could give her a piece of my mind, but I knew that would only make things worse, as good as it would feel to put her in her place.

Then my mind went to my earlier Instagram post. Had that picture of us caused all of this? My stomach roiled with guilt, but I tried not to think about it. I knew I hadn't done anything wrong. We were just friends. It's not like I'd been all over him or something.

No, if that picture had come up between them, then Bethany was using it as an excuse to dump Ian.

"Come on," I told Ian. "Forget about her. Let's have fun tonight and get your mind off of all that. At least for a little while." An idea came to mind, and I smiled. "And I know just the trick."

THREE

We walked into the living room, and I raised my voice. "Who's up for a game of truth or dare?" I yelled over the music with a huge smile on my face.

Ian leaned in toward me. "This is your idea of cheering me up?" he asked.

I clapped. "Of course!"

He plopped down on one of the couches with a look of blank resignation. "I guess it'll be entertaining watching you make a fool of yourself."

I laughed, not offended in the slightest. Ian making a joke was a really good sign, and I was only too happy to take one for the team.

Tori and Ella looked like they felt the opposite of excitement while Harper and Rey held back smiles.

But I knew something just a little crazy was what the doctor ordered for Ian. I might have gone for something like Spin the Bottle, but with flu season already starting, that was the last thing the boys and girls varsity teams needed right now.

Just about everyone gathered around the couches in the living room, and on my way to my seat, I whispered in Chris's ear about all of us cheering Ian up tonight and why. He gave me a quick nod.

My friends made room for me on the sofa, but when Noah walked in, Tori mumbled something about needing to talk to him somewhere else.

I knew she just wanted to get out of playing the game. "Fraidy cat!" I called after her.

It wasn't long before Ella and Jesse made the same type of excuse and huddled together in a corner of the room.

Harper's boyfriend, Emerson, put his arm around her, but at least they stayed.

Several minutes in, we were all laughing more than ever, even Ella and Jesse.

Chris had gotten a makeover, complete with lipstick and eyeshadow. I had to give it to him. He was always a good sport, on and off the field. Katie handed him several make-up wipes, still taking pictures.

Then Perry, the same girl who'd dared Chris to let her give him a makeover, had confessed that she'd pick Captain America out of all the Avengers to give her CPR if it came down to it.

I shook my head. "Thor, all the way. Or even better, Loki. There's something about a bad boy, don't you think?"

That made everyone laugh, and I winked at

Harper, who blushed profusely but giggled. Meanwhile, ever serious Emerson glanced away.

Next, it was my turn, and I was sure my smile reached my ears from the excitement.

Chris, finally make-up free, turned to me, and asked out loud, "Okay, Lena. Truth or dare?" he said with a quirk of his brow and a reckless grin.

I pretended to think about it, but I knew my answer wouldn't be a surprise. "Dare," I said, like it was a challenge.

Because it was.

Completing a good dare felt just like being on the soccer field and making an impossible shot. Or kissing for funsies.

I lived for the thrill of it.

Chris consulted with some of the other varsity boys, and Rey shook her head at me. "Girl, you are crazy," she whispered.

I smiled. "Just wait until it's your turn."

She gasped and covered her face with her journal so I could only see her eyes. "No way!" she said. "You know I can't handle this game. And especially not in public."

I winked at her and turned to Chris. "So? You got anything or what?" I said.

He finished whispering and met my gaze. "Oh, I've got something alright." His eyes practically twinkled with evil. "Lena, I dare you to kiss…" The room went completely silent waiting for him to finish that sentence. My heart beat like a drum in my chest. "Ian."

Uh, WHAT?

———

MY MOUTH ACTUALLY FELL OPEN. "WHAT?" I asked out loud.

I glanced at Ian, and he looked just as horrified as I felt.

I'd asked Chris to help me cheer up Ian, but this was not what I had in mind.

Chris high-fived his buddies, and I scoffed. "Chris! I can't kiss Ian. You know he's practically like a brother or something."

I looked to my friends for support, but they had been stunned silent because no one said anything. Neither did anyone else.

Probably because they knew Ian was the one guy I'd never kiss for funsies. We were friends, like real friends. And that was important to me.

But Chris only shrugged. "Sorry, Lena. Rules of the game. Either do the dare or lose."

He knew the magic word.

Lose.

Everyone on both teams knew I hated losing. Losing was the worst, and losing in front of everyone? I'd rather do anything else.

I sighed, knowing what I had to do.

Turning to Ian, I resigned myself to getting this dare done and over with.

Ian looked like he wasn't sure what to do. In fact, he resembled a deer in headlights.

He hugged a cushion to his chest like it was a bulletproof vest. "Uh…I don't know about this," he said.

Chris came over and said, "It's okay, man. This is just what you need. It's just for fun. It won't mean anything. Right, Lena?"

Everyone's head turned to me in one swift motion, and I took a deep breath. I looked at Ian. "It's just a dare," I said pasting on my best fake smile. "A quick peck on the lips, that's all."

He blinked back at me.

Then everyone began cheering and chanting, louder and louder until it was impossible to ignore. "KISS! KISS! KISS!"

Someone tapped my shoulder. It was Harper. "You know you guys don't have to do this if you don't want to," she said quietly.

"It's okay," I assured her. "It's just a game. Nothing more."

Besides, as of an hour ago, Ian no longer had a girlfriend so I had nothing to feel guilty about. No reason to say no.

I stood up, and so did Ian.

We walked over to the other side of the living room.

Ian stared back at me.

"Are you okay?" I said. "You know I'm just doing this on a dare, right? But we don't have to do this if you don't want to." I felt fine, but something told me he should hear Harper's words too.

He looked down, then at me again. I was sure the

continued chants of KISS, KISS, KISS weren't helping. "You're right. It's just a game. And I guess it could be worse."

I giggled, remembering the time someone had dared Chris to kiss his grandma on the lips at one of our soccer games last year.

Things could definitely be worse.

Ian still looked a little uneasy, but he stepped closer, leaning down toward me.

I pushed up on my toes so I could reach him, then I spotted a red Atlanta Hawks hat on one of the end tables nearby.

Just before Ian's lips reached mine, I snatched it and covered our faces.

Everyone groaned in disappointment, but I stifled a smile.

Ian's mouth pressed against mine, and his hand grazed my back and then pushed me closer to him.

The groans turned to loud cheers, but they were more like muffled noises in the background. I was too busy being surprised at how soft Ian's lips were and the feeling of my stomach doing several flips.

I stepped back, and so did Ian. It was over. Just like that.

The hat came down, and I turned to everyone and gave a bow, completely dazed. All I could focus on was the fact that kissing Ian had been really interesting.

And not quite like all those for funsies kisses I'd experienced before.

But I told myself it was just the high of both the

dare and the kiss. That was all…and why it had felt incredible.

Right?

Not because of his perfect smile, amazing hair, or strong hands.

NO.

FOUR

That stupid kiss wouldn't leave my thoughts alone the rest of the weekend, no matter how hard I tried.

But it was my fault for starting that game of truth or dare.

And also Chris's fault. Not one of his best ideas, daring me to kiss Ian.

Ugh.

Hopefully things would just go back to the way they were before. Well, not completely. I had my fingers crossed in hopes that Ian and Bethany wouldn't kiss and make up.

I just wanted to put that truth or dare kiss behind us, but at lunch on Monday, it was the only thing the #BFFs wanted to talk about.

Of course.

Tori eyed me like I was a puzzle she needed to figure out. "I don't know. That kiss seemed like more than just any old kiss. I could have sworn I saw literal sparks fly out from behind that hat."

Rey and Harper giggled.

Ella smiled. "What are you thinking?" she asked me.

I scoffed. "It was just a stupid dare. Otherwise, it never would have happened. I told you guys. We're just friends."

"Hmmm," said Tori in response. "You never know. A kiss could change everything, Lena."

"Oh yeah?" I asked. "Ian's not the first guy I've kissed for funsies."

Harper quirked a brow. "Every other guy wasn't Ian, though."

They stared at me, and I didn't say anything, thinking about Harper's comment.

Is that why I'd felt that funny feeling in my stomach? Because Ian was someone I knew and trusted? Because I'd felt a little something more?

Still… "He just got out of a relationship, though," I said. "I'm betting there's like an eighty percent chance he'll get back together with Bethany in no time. He's head over heels for her." Always had been, as far as I could tell. Ever since they'd started going out.

"Really?" Ella asked. "It's been the whole weekend. You'd think they would have made up by now if they were gonna get back together."

Rey nodded. "That's a good point."

"Besides," Tori said. "I heard she's already talking

to some other guy. Which frankly, isn't surprising. She doesn't usually stay single for long."

What? "Where'd you hear that?" I asked, pushing my full tray aside.

Tori picked at her salad. "This morning, on my way to math. One of Bethany's friends said she had gone out on a date with some college guy."

My stomach sank for Ian. This was going to crush him. "Are you sure?" I asked. But after what Ian had told me at the party, I couldn't say I was that surprised.

But I knew she wouldn't mention the rumor if she hadn't heard it herself.

She nodded. "Maybe it's for the best. Besides, you never know. You guys could end up becoming more than just friends."

It came out like a question, but one that she and everyone else wanted to know the answer to.

I already knew the answer, though. I shook my head. "No, I don't think so. I'm not even sure I see him like that, you know? We've been friends forever. Since middle school. I'm not sure I'd want to ruin what we have."

What we had was pretty good. I could count on Ian to be the shoulder I needed to lean on while we listened to music on the way to our next away soccer game or on the bleachers on the day of a home game. The person who gave me pointers during half time and gave me a pat on the shoulder whether we won or lost.

Rey's question brought me back to reality. "What

do you guys have?" she asked, pen poised above paper.

I shrugged. "We have…a real friendship."

Harper smiled. "Sometimes those turn into the best relationships."

"Maybe," I said, fidgeting with my napkin and shrugging my shoulders. "Maybe not. Anyway, he's totally heartbroken right now."

That door was closed. And always would be.

———

IAN and I shared a couple of classes, but we didn't really get to talk until after practice on Monday.

I let loose my long dark hair, pulled on an over-sized hoodie, and caught up to him on his way to his car. Everybody else peeled out of the parking lot, eager to get home.

"Hey," I called. We hadn't really talked since our kiss on Friday night, and I wanted to clear the air and find out if he was okay.

And if the rumors about Bethany were true.

Ian tossed his gym bag into his car and turned around. "Hey," he said, hardly looking at me.

I walked up to him, my hair blowing in the breeze. "I just wanted to ask how you're doing, you know, since…" I bit my lip, hoping he got the gist.

Ian leaned against his car, staring down at his feet. "Haven't you heard?" he asked quietly.

I leaned back against his car with him. "So it's true, huh?"

Clenching my jaw, I hated that Bethany had moved on just like that. What kind of person did that? It wasn't right.

Ian remained silent, and part of me wanted to take his hand. Then I reminded myself that we'd already crossed one line on Friday. No need to tiptoe toward it again so soon.

Or ever.

Ian exhaled. "I just—wish she'd give us another chance. I know she'd remember how good we are together."

But were you? I wanted to ask.

I grimaced, holding back my thoughts.

"After everything…" he said. "Almost two months."

I spoke carefully, not wanting to add to his pain. "Ian, maybe she's not worth all this heartbreak. You're such a good guy, and she's…"

"The girl I can't stop thinking about," he finished, staring off into the sky.

I shook my head. "I'm sorry, but she's a terrible person."

He shrugged and looked away. "There's more to her than you think."

I doubted that, but I decided not to voice my opinion on the matter. It'd probably just make him mad at me, and that was the last thing I wanted, for him to push me away. "Well, you're a total catch, Ian," I said, trying to put a smile on his face. "Don't forget that."

He only offered a small tight-lipped smile, a shadow of his usual grin.

"Hey, I don't say this to just anyone," I said, my heart beating a little quicker. "But you're a great kisser. And I think you know I'm quite experienced in this area."

Now he laughed, and I couldn't help but grin wide.

He looked at me. "It was hardly more than a peck, Lena. I'm not sure you could tell anything from that."

I continued teasing him. "Oh, I can tell," I said. "Believe me. If word gets out, which it very well could, that you're an amazing kisser, well, let's just say you'll have a line of girls ready to show you a good time like that." I snapped my fingers. "Maybe remind Bethany of what exactly she's missing out on."

His head snapped up. "You think so?"

I nodded. "Of course. Bethany's crazy to have given you up."

His eyes met mine, and I wondered if his stomach was doing somersaults too. "Lena," he breathed. "That's it."

Huh?

Ian stood up and faced me. "I want you to be my girlfriend," he said.

I faced him too. "Wh-what?" I asked, not sure I'd heard him correctly. Was I hearing right? For someone who usually thrived on going fast, all of a sudden I felt like I had whiplash.

"You can be my fake girlfriend," he said, a bright smile on his face. "Bethany will be so jealous, she'll realize she made a huge mistake. Plus she never did like you. You're the perfect candidate."

My mouth fell open, and I tried to process what I was hearing. "I'm not sure this is a good idea—" I started.

"It's a great idea," he said. "I should have thought of this sooner. At the party. I know for a fact that Bethany only told the school that she's going out with that dude because she got mad about our kiss. She'll go ballistic when she finds out that you're my girlfriend."

I shook my head. "Ian, we can't do this. We're just friends."

Just friends. Nothing more. No risk of losing Ian.

He grabbed my hands. "Come on, Lena. Just for a few days, maybe a couple weeks. I promise."

Ian's perfect—and hopeful—blue eyes stared back at me, waiting for me to say yes.

But I couldn't.

No, I said I wouldn't risk our friendship again.

But then he said the one thing he knew I couldn't refuse.

"Lena," Ian began. "I dare you to be my fake girlfriend."

FIVE

OH MY GOD.

How did one kiss on a dare turn into a fake relationship with one of my best friends?

I couldn't see a way out of it now that I'd agreed to it.

I only hoped that it would only last a few days and then Ian would get what he wanted—Bethany—even if I hated the very idea of those two getting back together.

Sure I had kissed a few boys for funsies here and there, but I'd never had a real boyfriend. I'd never really liked any guy quite enough for that. And now my first boyfriend was going to be Ian? A pretend relationship with my closest guy friend?

A lie?

Most of that night was spent tossing and turning —and freaking out—about the whole thing, but by the morning, I woke up with a whole new mindset.

So what if I had a fake boyfriend? I decided I

might as well have fun and roll with the whole thing. If anyone could pull this off, it was me.

When I walked into school, I did so with confidence and a deep breath. Time to find Ian, my new boo. According to his texts last night, he wanted to walk me to every one of my classes, spend lunch with me, and have the entire school know by the end of the day that we were a couple.

That was the plan.

I found Ian at his locker and tapped him on the shoulder.

He turned to me, a knowing smile forming on his face. "Good morning, babe," he said, shutting his locker and glancing around.

"Good morning, uh, handsome," I replied, cocking a brow playfully.

He held out his hand and exhaled. "Ready?" he asked.

"As I'll ever be," I said, forcing a smile.

He stared down at my hand, enveloped it with his, and led me toward my first class of the day. I tried not to think about how awkward it felt to walk with him like this. Would everybody see right through us?

Right away, students left and right stared or did double-takes as we passed by, clearly surprised by this new development.

Usually, I spent a few minutes before first period with the #BFFs, but today I was late as it was, and apparently, I'd have a new morning routine with Ian.

We arrived to my class and came to a stop. Ian

looked around nervously, like he wasn't sure what to do next.

Go in for a kiss? Peck on the cheek? Squeeze of the hand?

He settled for none of the above. Finally meeting my eyes, he said, "Uh, see you after class?"

"Sure," I said.

The warning bell rang, and he took off. I walked into class, where Tori and Ella were already waiting.

Tori glanced at the now empty doorway. "What was that?" she asked, the expression on her face somewhere between disbelief and excitement.

I sat down.

Ella leaned in. "Did we see things, or did you and Ian just—"

I nodded. "We're kind of a thing now."

Ella sat back in her chair like she was considering what I'd just said.

Tori laughed. "Kind of? What does that mean?"

I exhaled. "Well, he's kind of my boyfriend, as in…not really," I hinted.

Ella blinked. "Lena, you're not making any sense. I thought you said that kiss didn't mean anything?"

But Tori looked like she was starting to put two and two together.

I fiddled with a loose string on my shirt. "Like I said, he's not really my boyfriend…as in pretend…"

Ella gasped. "Pretend?" she said way too loudly.

I shushed her, and she clamped a hand over her mouth.

Tori shook her head and smiled. "Only you, Lena, would have a fake boyfriend."

"Fake's a strong word," I mumbled. "Besides, it's only to make Ian's ex jealous. If I have to kiss Ian for funsies a few times for that to happen, well, so be it." I gave them a wink and grin.

Ella laughed. "Goodness, Lena. Just be careful, though, okay?" she said.

The bell rang, and they faced forward. I did the same.

I leaned in toward her. "Nothing to be careful about," I assured her. "It's all pretend. I only agreed because of a stupid dare. Before I know it, Ian will be back with Bethany, and this will be over."

So I didn't like Bethany. But if Ian wanted to be with her, who was I to stop him?

Tori turned around and whispered, "I just hope it ends up being that simple."

———

AFTER SCHOOL, Ian held my hand and led me through the crowded hallways toward the soccer field.

What I didn't expect was to run into Bethany.

Somehow, we had successfully avoided her during every single class change earlier. I kept thinking we'd catch her walking toward us, maybe standing at someone's locker. I'd been ready for that first moment between us, to match her steely gaze or hurtful comment in a second.

But, of course, the instant I had relaxed and

forgotten all about her, she rounded the corner in front of us.

Ian immediately tensed up and dropped my hand. I grabbed it and held on, meeting Bethany's gaze head on.

She strode up to us, books held up to her chest and her long hair flowing down her shoulders.

Her eyes went from our clasped hands to Ian. "When I heard about you two becoming a thing, I said I wouldn't believe it until I saw it for myself." She paused. "And here we are." Bethany's voice dripped with venom.

Ian looked down at her. "Hey, Beth."

Her eyes narrowed. "Really, Ian? I can't believe you'd do this."

I scoffed. "That's rich, coming from you," I said.

Her head snapped toward me. But then her mouth curled into a smile. "Lena."

She turned back to Ian, placed her hand on Ian's arm, and I rolled my eyes, withholding a strongly-worded comment. "You look great, Ian. I'll text you later?"

I linked my elbow with his, holding on to his arm like I was drowning and he was my life raft. "Babe," I said loudly. "We're gonna be late for practice if we don't keep moving." I gave Ian a big kiss on the cheek and then flashed Bethany a smile. "Buh-bye now."

I didn't wait to check out Bethany's expression.

Hauling Ian behind me, I exhaled when he came back to his senses. "S-sorry about that. I wasn't expecting to see her," he confessed.

We turned the corner and stopped. I faced him. "She's gonna see through this in a millisecond if you practically drool over her like that every time."

Ian looked away sheepishly.

I focused my eyes on him, tone serious. "If you *really* want to make her jealous, we need to make this seem real. Because she didn't believe us for a second. I mean, did you see the way she looked at you?"

Ian blinked back at me, hope evident in his expression. "Do you think she still has feelings for me?"

I sighed. "Ian, I don't know. To me, it seems like she's just being possessive. Like she knows she can have you back in a heartbeat if she wants. But why would she already be dating some other guy if she really liked you? I'd never do that to someone I really cared about. And neither would you."

Just like that, Ian deflated again. "You're right," he said. He ran his hand through his hair. "Why are we even doing this? It's never going to work."

I bit my lip. "Because you're going to show her what she's missing out on. A truly great and caring guy. Who doesn't need someone like her."

He scoffed. "Is that even the kind of guy that girls want?" he muttered.

I put my hands on my hips. "Yes! Just look at my friends. Not one of their boyfriends are jerks. They're all nice guys. So no, nice guys don't always finish last."

He shrugged, not seeming convinced.

"Who knows," I tried. "Maybe she'll realize she

made a big mistake if she thinks we really are an item."

Ian looked up hopefully once more.

"And if not," I went on. "Then we're going to show her that you're better off without her. No moping around, okay?" I said, squeezing his arm with my hand.

He nodded. "See you at practice?" he asked.

"Sure thing," I said, getting the sense he wanted to be alone.

The #BFFs came up to me, then, backpacks over their shoulders. Tori shouldered a gym bag too.

She cocked a brow. "We saw Bethany. That was interesting."

I shrugged.

Harper came in close. "So is she like super jealous?"

We formed a tight-knit circle, staying out of everyone's way as much as possible.

I sighed. "I think so because she was all over him, but with Bethany, it's hard to tell if it's because she really likes him and wants to get back together with him or she just hates the idea of another girl claiming him so quickly. Especially me," I said.

Rey said, "What do you mean?"

I glanced around. "She always did hate the fact that we were pretty close. She never did like me. Which is fine because I've never been a fan of her either."

Ella nodded. "Does she like any girl, though?

Even her friends seem more like they're just accessories to her."

I agreed. "I know, right?" I shook my head. "I just hope he realizes that he's way too good and pure for her. Deserves way better, if you ask me."

Tori smiled. "We think so too." She winked at me, and I knew what she was trying to imply.

But instead of addressing that, I eyed my phone and said I was late for soccer practice.

The whole way down to the field, though, I couldn't get Bethany's smug face out of my mind.

SIX

"Lena, why didn't you say anything?" Samantha practically shrieked when I entered the girls' locker room.

I knew it was only a matter of time before the rest of the team found out, but I didn't think they'd be so ecstatic about the news.

Katie came up to me. "Girl, I don't know if I should be jealous or happy for you." She wrapped me in a hug. "Just kidding. So jelly, but still so happy for you two."

Samantha gave me a wink. "I guess that truth or dare kiss really turned into something, huh?" She gave me a wide grin.

Even as we made our way to the field, the chatter wouldn't stop.

And of course, I had to go along with it, letting the girls know how excited I was to be with Ian too.

According to them, I'd snatched him right up, without giving any of the rest of the girls a chance.

But what could I say? It's not like I could let them in on the secret.

If this was going to work, I had to make sure that no one else found out the truth. Ian was counting on me, as much as I hated the reason this was even happening.

Perry dribbled her ball at her feet on the grass. "I knew you two would end up becoming more than just friends."

Katie rolled her eyes. "Did not."

"Did so," Perry argued. "I always thought he had a thing for you last year, Lena. And why he stayed single for so long."

I scoffed. "I don't think so."

Usually, I was pretty good at reading that kind of vibe from guys, and Ian had not been sending them. Nope.

If anything, Ian seemed to be one of those guys that just didn't give off those vibes. He'd never been one to confess crushes or make comments about how hot a girl was. At least not to me.

I assumed he talked about it on some level with the guys. Or maybe grunted. Who knows. I just always thought he was being respectful or something.

But secretly crushing on me? No way. Not possible.

Sam nudged me. "I just think you guys are like the most adorable couple ever."

The other girls murmured in agreement as we began stretching.

Sam went on. "And with Homecoming coming up

in a few weeks—oh, you guys have to coordinate your outfits and everything!" She clapped with excitement.

I shook my head. "Simmer down over there. This relationship is like a couple days old. No need to start thinking about Homecoming. Besides, you never know…" That sentence trailed off, and Katie gave me an odd look. I shrugged. "I mean, next you're gonna want us to pick out china patterns or something."

Samantha's mouth fell open like she was perplexed and didn't know quite how to respond to my exasperated comment.

Thankfully, Coach blew his whistle precisely at that moment, immediately shifting everyone's attention on him. "Okay, everyone. Five laps with your ball. You know the drill," he said, checking something off on his clipboard.

The boys and girls varsity soccer teams practiced together a lot of the time. Especially since we shared the same coach and assistant coach.

We warmed up together, we ran through countless drills together, and sometimes we even scrimmaged together.

Today was no different.

I tossed my ball a few feet in front of me and began dribbling around the field, ignoring the looks of the guys and girls at me and Ian.

Now was time for business, not laughing or gossiping. Everyone knew I loved to goof off on the bus or after a game-winning goal, but never during practice.

Even if my pretend boyfriend was a few feet away.

While I waited in line during a passing drill,

though, one of the senior guys, Miguel, came up to me. "So it's true, Lena? You're off the market? I thought you didn't do the boyfriend thing?" he said with a smile and a wink.

Miguel had asked me out before. We may or may not have kissed during junior year, but that didn't mean I wanted to date the guy. It was totally for funsies. He just hadn't gotten the message.

I shrugged, too focused on the assistant coach about to throw me the soccer ball to come up with a coherent response.

He hissed playfully like he'd been burned on the chest. "Ouch. Talk about burn. Well, if you end up needing a date to Homecoming, you know where to find me."

I scoffed, keeping my eye on the ball coming towards me. My foot stopped it perfectly on the grass. Without a second glance at Miguel, I said loudly, "Keep on dreaming."

Several of the guys snickered, but I was already off.

Sure, boys were cute, but my first love was soccer, and there wasn't any boy that would change that.

Not even this fake relationship with Ian. Besides, we both knew it wouldn't last.

And I was fine with that.

———

MY FAVORITE PART of practice was the scrimmage

at the end. I threw on a maroon penny, ready to kick the yellow team's butt.

Scrimmage or not, I liked to win. Or at least give it my all.

My dad always said you could walk off the field with your head held high if you gave it your best, no matter how badly you lost.

"There will always be someone who is better than you, Lena. It's a good reminder to stay humble. Do not forget that," he would say. I could hear his voice in my head just as if he was standing right next to me.

But that didn't mean I didn't like to win.

And I especially liked beating the boys. I wasn't sure most of them knew the meaning of the word humble, and it was always nice to give them a nice heaping serving of it on the rare occasion the girls could win.

Ian stood under the net across the grassy field.

There was a chill in the air, but we no longer felt it. Instead, sweat continued to drip down my neck and forehead.

The boys were winning two to one, and I was determined to make another goal after the one that had just gotten past our defense.

Chris winked at me from a few feet away. He was a forward, which meant he was fast. His job was to shoot. Same as me.

Beyond him, Miguel stood as sweeper. The main defending player. I had to get past him to take a shot at their goal. And then I had to hope that Ian wouldn't be good enough to stop it.

41

He'd already blocked a couple of really great shots. Ian was an even better goalkeeper than he was last year.

The whistle blew, and I kicked the ball forward to Katie. The two teams battled back and forth for a few minutes, but eventually, we made it near the goal.

Samantha passed the ball to me. Miguel wouldn't get to me in time.

This was my chance.

Out of the corner of my eye, I saw Ian getting into position to block whatever I was about to send his way.

With a quick glance at the right bottom corner of the goal, I ran toward Ian and the goal he was protecting.

He was just a few feet away now, and my lungs burned and my legs felt like they were on fire. But, giving it everything I had left, I kicked the ball toward the right corner.

Ian lunged, diving for the ball.

Barely nudged it with his gloved fingers, but it was enough. The ball hit the right post and bounced away.

But my eyes stayed on Ian. Something was wrong.

He wasn't getting up. He usually had the reflexes of a cat, but now, he remained on the ground.

I ran over to him.

Kneeling beside him, I asked, "Oh my gosh, I'm so sorry. Are you okay?"

He moved so he was on his side, and his hand

went to his knee. "I think I'm okay. Just banged up." Meeting my eyes, he said, "That was a good shot."

I smiled. "You stopped it."

We looked to his knee, and Miguel and Samantha joined us.

It was scraped pretty bad, but luckily, it didn't look too serious. "I think you're gonna live," I teased.

Coach came over, and he clutched at his chest in relief when he heard it was just a scrape. "Get it taken care of," he said. "You know where the first aid kit is."

Miguel helped Ian up, who put his weight on the opposite knee.

I grabbed his arm, helping him stand steady. "I'll go with you."

I led Ian off the field and toward the locker room.

Chris called to us. "You two better be back in five minutes," he teased.

Ian looked sheepishly at me, and I rolled my eyes. "When do you think the teasing and talk will stop?" I asked as we walked into the locker room.

Ian sat down on one of the benches, and I went for the first aid kit.

He said, "I don't know. I didn't think us going out would end up being such a big deal."

I sat down next to him and opened the first aid kit, grabbing some hydrogen peroxide and swabs. "Yeah, me too."

"You are a catch," he said. "I mean, how many guys have asked you out?" he said with a smile.

I scoffed. "Whatever."

I didn't quite know what else to say without things becoming awkward.

When he didn't say anything, I looked up, staring into his bright blue eyes for a second too long, my heart beating like I was chasing a ball instead of hardly moving. Blinking rapidly, I focused on Ian's knee again.

Then I dabbed his knee with the hydrogen peroxide swab.

But I couldn't get that thought off my mind. Everyone being surprised about us and yet also saying they should have seen it coming all along.

I wondered how much truth there was in that. I couldn't quite make sense of it. The thought of Ian and me for real felt weird, like a pair of socks that didn't quite match.

Or eating pizza with fries. Fries belonged with burgers, not pizza.

Ian and I were like that. Two opposites who had somehow become close friends.

He was quiet and humble. A nice guy.

Meanwhile, I was loud and crazy and said things I often regretted.

No way we belonged together.

No way.

SEVEN

After I patched both of us up, Ian and I hobbled back to practice but not for long.

The previously gray sky had turned dark, and pretty soon, fat drops of cold rain hit us full force.

Coach blew his whistle, but both teams were already picking up cones like madmen and madwomen. We raced back to the shelter of the locker rooms, grins on our faces.

Practice had ended half an hour early, a rare treat.

After we grabbed our stuff, the girls and guys buzzed about going out to eat and hanging out before going home.

Katie called from her car, "Shake Shack, everyone? See you there!" Several people waved or called back as they ran in the rain toward their cars. Then Katie rolled up her window and drove off.

Using my hand to shield my eyes from the pouring rain, I looked for Ian and saw him climbing into his car a few feet away. Wondering if he was heading to the Shake Shack too, I ran over to his car and hopped in on the front passenger side, dropping my gym bag at my feet.

Surprise etched his face. "Hey," he said.

"Hey," I replied. "You joining everyone else? What's the plan?"

He didn't say anything for a second, just stared at something on his phone.

I cocked a brow. "You know, we're supposed to be boyfriend girlfriend now. In fact," I said, settling back into the seat and getting comfortable, "you really should be driving me everywhere. That would be the right thing to do, you know," I teased.

But his grim expression remained. He showed me what was on his phone, and my smile faltered.

An Instagram post of Bethany and some older looking guy, both of them looking pretty cozy.

Ian tossed his phone on the dash with a heavy sigh. Then he stared out the windshield, at the rain-drops hitting the glass. His eyes traced the rain running down in streams in front of him.

"I'm really sorry," I said quietly.

He bit his lip, shaking his head. "Just...I miss Bethany." His fingers grazed his hair before he put his hands on the steering wheel and he leaned forward. "How can she just move on like that? I don't get it."

He looked at me like I might have the answer, but I had nothing. Nothing that would help him feel better anyway.

After a minute of just listening to the rain patter

on his car, I put my hand on his arm, I said, "You're gonna get through this, you know. No matter what."

"We were supposed to go to Homecoming together," he said.

"I'll go with you," I said, and my stomach got this weird feeling as I heard the words come out of my mouth. "Who cares if we're still doing this dare or not. I'm going to make sure you have a great time. No staying home alone to mope and eat junk food."

A small smile finally cracked his face. "But why? That sounds so much better." He looked at me.

"Nope," I said, smiling back, glad he was goofing off with me now. "We're going to get all dressed up and have a great time, me and you. And I'm sure you'll have a long line of girls wanting to dance with you."

Now his grin grew a little bigger, and just seeing it made me feel like all was right in the world again. "Nah, I just want to hang out with you."

I gave him my best smile back, ignoring the somersault my stomach did just then. "So what about grabbing a bite with everyone? Do you want to go? Feed me French fries in front of everyone, maybe?" I wiggled my brows up and down so he could clearly see how enticing this offer was.

But he deflated like a balloon.

"Sorry, Lena," he said. "I'm not sure I'm up for it. Maybe we can pretend we're hanging out on our own or something. But I think I just want to go home. It's been a tough day."

I nodded, trying to understand and not pout.

Hanging out with everyone would have been fun, but the cute French fry thing would have to wait.

He tried to smile but faltered. "Walk you to your car?" he asked. The rain began coming down hard again.

I sat up. "No, thanks. Even if you could use a shower. See you tomorrow?" I said, my hand on the door.

He gave a quick nod, sticking his key in the ignition. "Yeah."

Pushing the door shut behind me, I ran back to my car in the rain.

When his car pulled away, I stared after it, wishing Ian would forget all about Bethany.

And go back to being the Ian I used to know.

———

THAT NIGHT, after a hot shower and getting into my favorite pair of pajamas, I turned on the TV in my room.

I looked for my go-to post-practice veg show: Friends.

A few minutes later, Ross screamed, "WE WERE ON A BREAK!"

Usually Ross cracked me up, but tonight, all I could think about was Ian and how upset he'd been earlier.

No way were we going to keep up the charade for long.

This whole thing had been a bad idea.

My phone went off, and I picked it up.

Ella's picture appeared on my phone. I tapped the green button and her face smiled back at me. Then Rey's.

I gave a wave. "Hey, guys. What's up?"

Tori and Harper popped in too.

Ella looked like she was in her room, laying on her own bed. "Well, you guys, I was thinking. We're a few months into senior year—"

Tori gave a small scream. "Can't believe it!"

"Me neither," Harper said with a smile.

Ella laughed. "I was thinking, we really need to start thinking about—"

" Our senior prank?" I guessed loudly.

Ella furrowed her brow. "—submitting our college applications."

I groaned loudly. "I should have known this was the reason for your video call. You are such a *nerd*," I said, laughing.

Tori cracked up too. "In a good way."

Harper spoke up, nodding. "Definitely in a good way. I'm so going to need your help, Ella. I have no idea what I'm supposed to do or where I should apply."

Rey raised her hand. "Same. Help."

I was way too tired to even think about something like college right now. "Ella, we all know you already have like a full ride to whatever school you want. How about you just fill out my applications for me?" I gave her a sweet smile, but she shook her head. "Besides, I can hardly think about college right now."

Rey said, "Too busy thinking about the new boyfriend, huh?" She winked.

I scoffed. "Hardly. Except that he's just not being himself. He got upset after Bethany posted a picture of her with her new beau or whatever."

Harper blinked back at me. "He's taking the breakup hard, huh?" she asked.

I nodded. "I guess I didn't really think about that when I agreed to this whole thing."

They didn't say anything so I kept talking, thinking out loud really.

"I just wish he realized the fact that he's too good for her. Ugh." I stared up at the ceiling, hating how my voice sounded saying those words out loud. And how they made me feel.

Harper brought me back to the conversation. "It must be hard watching him go through all this when you guys have been friends for a while. I bet you're torn between telling him how you feel and just being there for him."

How did she always know the right thing to say? It had to be a gift. "Exactly. Like he begged me to do this. I couldn't say no. But at the same time, I hate that I'm helping him get her back."

I turned over and buried my face into my pillow, holding my phone up with my hand so my friends could see just how torn I was.

When I was done venting my frustrations into my pillow, I found my friends staring back at me.

Tori bit her lip. "Are you sure that's the only reason you're upset?"

"What do you mean?" I asked.

She shook her head. "Nothing."

Ella started talking about college applications again.

Meanwhile, I wondered how I was going to get through the rest of this fake relationship.

Part of me wondered if I'd come out of it in one piece, but I immediately thought: why wouldn't I?

EIGHT

The only thing on my mind the next day at school, though, was how Ian had done a complete one-eighty.

He was no longer extra quiet or obviously heart-broken like before.

Instead, he seemed to be back to his old self. And really taking his role as my fake boyfriend seriously.

On our way to lunch, he insisted we talk about the things we were each required to do.

"I'll keep walking you to class," he said. "That's expected."

I observed the way he bit the inside of his mouth as he thought. "But you'll be late to Science if you do that. It's across campus from my second period."

"So? I'll run. That's what a good boyfriend does," he said, wagging his brows.

I laughed. "Well, just be careful. Don't run over any poor freshmen on your way to class."

"Will do." He paused. "Or won't do," he said. I

giggled. He snapped his fingers. "And we should write notes and stuff. Not just the usual texting. We should go old school, don't you think?" He waited for me to respond, his expression full of hope and enthusiasm. I tried to guess why.

Was he just really serious about making Bethany jealous? Was this his way of moving on? Having fun while he was at it?

I nodded as we walked. "Okay. We can slip them into each other's lockers."

"Yeah, good idea. Or I can slip them into your back pocket." Was that a mischievous twinkle in his eye?

I stopped. "Slip them into my back pocket?" I asked, raising my brows.

He shrugged, a growing smile on his face. "Sure. If you don't mind."

Not sure how I felt about that, I said, "Hm, I'll get back to you on that."

We arrived at the cafeteria, and he held out his hand. I took it, not quite sure how I felt about walking in with him, hands held.

Then I reminded myself that this was just a game, a dare. Just a role I was playing.

We got in line, and I glanced around.

But Ian was still brainstorming ideas. "I can drive you home too, you know? After practice."

"What about my car?" I asked. I'd just gotten it a few months ago, and I liked driving it. Especially to school in the mornings. "I really don't want to take the bus to school."

But he had an answer ready. "I'll pick you up in the morning," he whispered with a smile, leaning in close like he was telling me a big secret.

"Pick me up?" I asked. I knew for a fact that he used to pick up Bethany every morning, and there came that weird feeling in my stomach again.

He nodded. "Maybe we can pick up coffee? Skip the one-star breakfast here and grab some real food instead?"

Coffee? Breakfast? "Now you're talking," I said.

He handed me a tray, letting me go first in line.

I grabbed a sandwich here, an apple there, thinking about everything Ian was saying.

It sounded like life as Ian's girlfriend could be pretty good.

I always knew that Ian was a gentleman. Respectful, nice, always opened a door for you. But I didn't realize how romantic he was too.

Writing notes to each other? I had no idea what I would say, but I guess it didn't matter.

It was all just a show, right?

We reached the end of the line, where the lunch lady at the cash register waited for me to pay up, and I glanced back at Ian. "What? You're not paying for my lunch?"

A look like realization hit his face, and he set his tray down and reached for his wallet.

He could not be serious. "I'm kidding!" I said with a laugh. "Sheesh."

I was still laughing about it a minute later when I set my tray down at the #BFF table. Ian was right beside me. The girls gave him a wave, and he gave a cool, "Hey."

Then he turned to me. I expected him to say he'd see me later or something.

What I didn't expect was for him to lean down and kiss me on the forehead.

Or the way my stomach flipped when he did it. In front of the entire lunchroom.

But I couldn't help but smile. At least this version of Ian, the sweet and doting kind, was way better than the one from yesterday afternoon.

I finally sat down, my gaze on the girls.

Ella smiled. "That was just about the cutest thing I've ever seen."

Tori eyed me. "Lena, is that a subtle blush, I see?" she asked, amused.

The other #BFFs giggled.

"No," I insisted, throwing a French fry at her.

But maybe they were right.

Ian was my friend, sure. But he was also pretty handsome.

And he'd just kissed me. What girl in her right mind wouldn't blush?

Right?

———

HAVING Ian pick me up for school was weird.

By the time, he got there, my parents were already off for work, so I waited on the steps of our porch.

A few minutes later, his shiny navy blue Mazda pulled in, and I raised a brow. Very nice.

Way nicer than my sensible used '05 Honda sitting in the driveway.

Why couldn't my parents get me a car like this?

I strode up to the car, but Ian was already there, with the door open. I smiled. "You don't have to do this. No one's around."

He winked. "Good morning to you too."

After that, we stopped at the drive-thru for breakfast and coffee, as promised.

I was very impressed.

And cruising while Ian took the wheel definitely beat having to get to school while dodging morning traffic.

By first period, I was perfectly chipper and in a great mood. It was probably the coffee talking, but it sure felt like the start of a great day.

Not even Bethany's most annoyed facial expression could ruin it, try as she might in between classes.

I was pretty sure I saw her actually fume when Ian slipped me a note in front of our lockers before our last class of the day.

It was great.

When I sat down and the teacher started handing back last week's homework, I unfolded it.

Ian's small yet neat handwriting stared back at me.

Roses are red.
Violets are blue.

You're pretty cute
And I wish that you knew

Haha. Best I could do. What do you think? ;)

-Ian

I laughed out loud, but a curious look from the teacher had me putting my hand over my mouth and hiding Ian's note under my notebook.

But not before stealing one last look at the misshapen heart he'd drawn at the bottom of the paper.

The entire note looked like a second grader had written it. But it was just about the cutest thing I'd ever gotten.

No matter how hard I tried, I couldn't stop smiling like I'd just won a million dollars the rest of the period.

By the end of soccer practice, Ian and I made our way back to his car. We waved goodbye to everyone else, and once again, he had the car door open for me.

He got inside too.

"That note you sent me," I said. "Cheesiest thing ever."

He stopped, letting his keys hang from the ignition. "You liked it?"

I laughed. "Sure," I replied. But then I saw the way his face lit up. "I sure did. Have you always been such a die-hard romantic?"

He shrugged. "It's what any good boyfriend does, right?" Then he started up the car, and we left the school in silence.

Ian was probably right. Little things like that. It was what any good boyfriend would do. That didn't mean most boyfriends did those little things. Send notes. Open car doors. Take me home.

No wonder Ella, Tori, and Harper were always so gaga over their boyfriends. It felt like Christmas had come early. Or I'd scored the game-winning goal at the state championship.

All the time.

And this wasn't even real.

I couldn't imagine what the real thing would be like.

Sending each other gooey texts and kissing emojis. Being practically glued to each other.

I'd never really liked the idea of having a boyfriend, at least not enough to give up my total independence. Just doing whatever I wanted whenever I wanted.

But maybe I just hadn't met the right guy yet.

Whenever I did have a boyfriend for real, I decided he needed to be like Ian.

NINE

Ian pulled into my parking lot, right behind my Dad's Toyota.

Dad was home early.

I grabbed my book bag and gym bag, ready to thank Ian for the ride home.

Except Ian's face had turned white. I looked to where he'd fixed his stare, seeing my dad slip out the front door.

"Don't worry," I said with a laugh. "It's just my dad."

His eyes only grew wider. "That's exactly why I'm trying not to freak out here. I've never met a—uh…"

I was pretty sure I understood what he was trying to say, so I nodded. "Don't worry. He won't bite." I opened the door. "I think," I said carefully. Then I giggled to myself.

Ian stepped out too. "Are you sure?" he muttered.

But it was too late for me to answer.

My dad made his way down the porch steps

quickly, his mouth slightly turned down and his eyes completely serious.

"Hey, dad," I greeted, but Dad's eyes weren't on me. They were on a wide-eyed, slightly shaky Ian.

For someone who towered a good foot, foot and a half, above my Dad, Ian sure did look nervous. I held back a smile.

Ian held out his hand. "Hi. I mean, good afternoon, sir. My name is Ian."

Ian looked at me like he wasn't sure what he should do next. He was probably wondering just how much English my dad knew.

I walked up to them both so that we formed an odd sort of triangle.

"*Mija, quien es este muchacho?*" Dad asked me quietly in Spanish, his gaze never leaving Ian.

"Dad, this is Ian. He's on the boy's varsity soccer team. He plays goalkeeper. You've seen him," I explained in Spanish.

My dad eyed him closely, looking him up and down.

Ian glanced back at me.

Dad nodded slowly, just barely. Then he grunted. "Is he…?" he asked quietly.

How to answer that question…I'd never really thought about what I'd tell my parents. It's not that I wasn't allowed to have a boyfriend. I suppose they just expected more of a heads up.

Oops.

Probably should have thought this through.

"Uh, yeah, I guess," I said in Spanish.

Not understanding at all what I'd just said, Ian gave my dad a small smile, but now my dad looked as serious as a heart attack. Ian took a step back, smile gone.

I gave him a wave. Probably better to go inside now and call it a night. "See you tomorrow?" I called.

He waved but was already opening his car door. Ian looked like he couldn't leave fast enough. I made a mental note to tease him about it endlessly tomorrow.

My dad and I went inside, and I closed the front door behind me.

My mom stood at the window, peeking out through the blinds. "Lena, who was that?" she asked, hardly tearing her eyes away from our driveway and Ian's quickly departing car.

"Ian," I said. "He's nice. And super talented."

She turned to me, hands on her hips. "Did you ride home with him? You know you're not allowed to ride in boys' cars, Lena."

But I was already on my way to my room. "So what's for dinner?" I called.

My mom would probably never let me hear the end of this, but I knew that riding in Ian's car was definitely no big deal. It's not like we were making out or anything.

Really, we were just friends.

Nothing more.

THE BALL SOARED DOWN toward me, a dark shadow against the sunlight. The chilly fall air bit at my cheeks.

I took a step back to get in front of the ball but not far enough. I widened my arms and leaned back, the ball hitting my chest and then falling at my feet.

"Good," my dad called.

I dribbled around the cones, cutting this way then that, my feet pounding the grass under me.

About a dozen feet in front of the goal, my foot connected with the ball, sending it in a neat arc toward the net.

It went in just below the left corner.

The corners were my sweet spot, and I loved them because they were almost impossible for the opposing goal keeper to reach.

Which meant the ball would be near impossible to block.

I came to a stop and looked toward my dad. His hands behind his back, he nodded in approval. "Again," he said.

I did it again and again and again, the ball landing inside the net nine times out of ten.

Then ball control drills. Sprints.

Two hours of practice until my lungs screamed for me to stop and catch my breath. When my dad raised his hand, I knew I could stop for a break. I collapsed on the grass.

It was just me and my dad today, like most Saturdays. Unless one of us was sick or the weather was too harsh, we spent Saturday mornings out here, ever since I could remember.

These practices with my dad were the reason I made the girls' varsity team sophomore year and could keep up with most of the boys.

I just hoped the hard work paid off and I could score a scholarship to college. Maybe play on the US women's Olympic team some day?

That would be wild.

Just the thought of it had me smiling up towards the sun.

I stood up, grabbed my water bottle, and took a drink.

Dad walked over. "Keep playing like that, and those schools will have no choice but to ask you to play for them," he said.

I beamed. He didn't usually compliment me like that, so I stored his words away like a prized possession.

My foot on the ball in front of me, I said, "Coach says there will be scouts showing up at our big game in a couple of weeks." With the team's perfect record so far, they were definitely interested in our top players.

The question was: would they be interested in me?

If I could keep playing like I had the past couple games, I would definitely have a shot.

No matter what, I couldn't mess up my chances.

After all the hard work I'd put in, I was counting on my soccer career *not* ending after high school.

IT HAD BEEN a week and a half since this dare had started, and I wondered just how much longer it was going to go on.

It wasn't that I wasn't having fun because I definitely was. There were perks to having a boyfriend, it seemed.

Big perks, like getting picked up for school and then dropped off after practice. Ian bought me a coffee or breakfast on some mornings, if I could run out of the house in time.

But what I loved the most about being his pretend girlfriend was having a monopoly on Ian.

No more Bethany texting or calling him before games, after practice, and any time we happened to hang out together.

I actually got to talk to Ian during the school day too. We had lunch together, but he knew that was my #BFF time. Every time he kissed me on the forehead before leaving, though, it reminded me of how things could be. If we kept this up.

Or if he at least stayed single.

It was a lot of fun getting to hang out with my best friend—who happened to be very easy on the eyes—all the time.

Ian got me. He made me laugh. Made me feel better right before a big soccer game.

"You got this," he'd assure me before I walked out onto the field.

We hadn't lost a single game yet, and I knew

that it wasn't just due to practicing non-stop during the week and on the weekends at home with my dad.

Ian helped me keep my head on straight.

I wasn't sure what I'd do when our game was up, and then some other girl inevitably came along to take him away from me.

Which is why I wasn't expecting him to level up our fake relationship.

For some reason, he always shared these ideas in the lunch line.

He stood close, really close, and I reminded myself that it was to keep up the charade. "You know, I was thinking," he began.

I smiled. "Uh oh," I said. "Be careful. You could hurt yourself."

He nudged me playfully, and I giggled. His eyes turned serious again. "I was thinking...You know that big game on Friday?"

"Uh huh," I said, wondering why the lunch line wasn't moving. Maybe they were out of French fries. Today was chicken sandwich day. They could not be out of French fries already.

Ian kept talking, unaware of the potential dilemma. "Well, I was thinking that..."

I wished he would spit it out. I turned to him, wondering what he was trying to say.

My style was to just rip off the bandaid, but clearly, Ian didn't have the same approach.

"Maybe," he went on slowly, and I nodded just as slowly. "Maybe we could sit together and—"

"Ian," I said with a laugh. "You know we always sit together."

He glanced away before his gaze met mine again. "I know, but maybe this time, we could, you know, sit together as a couple."

I furrowed my brow, not understanding what he was saying. "We have been sitting together as a couple."

He bit his lip. "I mean, like—it's an hour and a half long trip. I thought we could bring each other's favorite snacks, maybe you can nap on my shoulder…" His voice faded then, and I could tell he was carefully gauging my reaction.

A grin slowly grew on my face. Then I laughed, not exactly sure why.

The hope on his face disappeared. "Sorry, I know. It's dumb. Just forget I said it." He shoved his hands in his pockets, and I could practically see him trying to disappear.

I put my hand on his arm. "Ian, I don't think it's dumb. You just caught me off guard."

He looked at me. "You sure?"

"Yeah," I replied. "Let's do it." I leaned in close. "We are a couple after all."

He grinned, and the line finally began moving. "It'll be fun," he said. "We can make the whole thing cheesy, take some pictures."

I nodded. "Yeah," I replied, loving how excited he was for this. For some reason, though, my stomach turned. Was it hot in here or was it just me?

When we got our trays, I looked for the French

fries. There they were. Ian handed me the container. "Thanks," I said, hardly meeting his eyes.

The truth was the whole thing had just turned a little scary. Holding hands and walking together? Saying mushy things in public every once in a while? Spending more time together? I didn't mind any of that. It was fun. Or sometimes even funny.

But resting my head on Ian's shoulder and falling asleep? Letting our bodies touch? That was ten times scarier than our truth or dare kiss ever would be.

I had definitely not signed up for this.

And I wasn't sure how I felt about it.

The butterflies in my stomach made me feel nervous, like maybe this fake relationship was becoming a little too real.

Which meant the risk was real.

The question was: could I handle it?

TEN

On Friday the boys and girls' varsity teams were called to the gym just after lunch. We had a long bus ride ahead of us before our game tonight.

We didn't usually have far away games, but when we did, I always looked forward to them because it meant we got to miss class.

Instead of sitting in a classroom with twenty-five other kids listening to a boring lecture, I got to hang out on a bus, listen to music, and goof around with Ian and everyone else instead.

As I made my way to the gym, my phone buzzed with a text.

Ella: Good luck today! Don't worry. I'll take notes for you. We can review them together this weekend :)

I held back a smirk.

Oh, Ella.

I typed out a quick message before hopping on the bus.

Lena: Oh I'm not worried. LOL. Thanks! I'll get them from you next week. But I can't study this weekend. Lots to do :)

Ella sent a blank expression emoji.

Tori: Let me guess. Kicking a ball, watching hours of TV, and sleeping in?

Lena: How'd you know? ;)

Ella, Harper, and Rey started making plans to look at college websites tomorrow so I began browsing social media instead.

My bags were at the front of bus with everyone else's stuff, but right now my seat was empty except for me.

It wasn't long before Ian arrived. I stood up and let him slide by. He liked the window seat so he could stare outside, while I liked to go from seat to seat so I could talk to the rest of the team, as much as it annoyed our bus driver.

But today would be different.

A couple nights ago, Ian had texted me so we could actually make plans for today. I told him I'd bring a blanket and some snacks. He wouldn't tell me what he was going to bring.

Just sent a winking emoji, which had me wondering what he was up to.

Ian was way too good at this boyfriend thing.

And it scared me a little.

Now I had my fleece blanket in my lap, perfect for warding off the chill in the air but not for keeping two best friends just that. Friends.

A warm smile lit up Ian's face next to me. He had

a small bag with him, the kind colleges and businesses gave away for free all the time.

I covered his legs with half of my blanket, realizing I needed to scoot in closer to him. Maybe I should have brought a bigger blanket.

But he didn't seem to mind.

I wondered what was inside the bag, which sat on his lap. "What's that?" I asked.

"You'll see," he replied. "Close your eyes."

I eyed him. "I'm not sure if I trust you."

He laughed. "You're my girlfriend, aren't you?" he said loudly. Then his voice became softer. "Don't you trust me?"

We were not strangers to pulling practical jokes on each other. Mostly me on him, but still.

I closed my eyes anyway, wondering what he was going to do.

"Open your mouth," he said.

I opened my mouth to complain, but then something salty and warm hit my tongue.

Recognizing the taste immediately, I opened my eyes and confirmed it. "You brought French fries?" I asked in disbelief. "How are these still warm?" I grabbed a few more, then took the whole thing.

He smiled, clearly proud of himself. "Ran out and grabbed them during lunch just now."

No wonder I hadn't seen him. "Clever," I said, stuffing my mouth with more fries. "Just don't do this every game because I won't be scoring goals for much longer if I have these too often."

I glanced to the front of the bus. Coach would kill

me if he saw me eating junk before a big game. But I couldn't stop eating the fries.

Savoring them. "Yum," I said. "You win boyfriend of the year," I said.

I gave him the fries to hold and pulled out some sour gummy worms from my book bag. I knew they were his favorite. In fact, I loved them too.

"For you," I said.

He opened the bag right away, but instead of popping one in his mouth, he held it up. "Want one?" he asked, wiggling his eyebrows. Every time he did that, it made me laugh and today was no different.

I let him feed me, taking the gummy worm from his fingers gently with my mouth.

"Ew," I heard behind me. It was Katie. "I don't know if you guys are completely adorable or just gross. Maybe both," she finished.

Samantha giggled behind her.

Chris came up behind them and looked our way. "What are you two doing?" He saw the snacks in our laps. "Oh wow. You two are gonna be that old couple that wears like the same sweater and stuff and does everything together, aren't you?" he joked.

"Maybe," I replied, sounding defensive but not really.

I glanced back at Ian, and he had this weird look on his face.

Finally, Samantha, Katie, and Chris kept moving and found their own seats.

"So what else did you bring?" I asked Ian.

He pulled out a bag of chocolate kisses and a red Gatorade. My favorite flavor.

"Maybe we should save them for after the game," he said sheepishly.

I giggled. "Good call. I'm not gonna be able to run at all if you keep feeding me."

He laughed, and the sound of it reached all the way to my belly.

Ian pulled out his phone and his earbuds. "Maybe we can listen to some music instead. I added a few songs to the playlist. Wanna listen?"

I nodded, and he scooted in close again, our shoulders and legs touching.

The bus rumbled to life, and everyone kind of quieted down.

Ian gave me an earbud, and I slipped it into my ear.

The first song was different. His playlist contained loud, upbeat music to get us in the mood to play. And win.

This was like that. Except it was also a love song.

After a while, I settled into Ian's shoulder. This time, though, he put his arm around me, and I ignored how hard my heart beat against my rib cage.

The more we sat like that, the more right it felt, even if my heart didn't want to get it together.

And falling asleep on Ian's shoulder, with his head resting atop of mine?

Not as scary as I thought.

———

WITH HOMECOMING RIGHT around the corner, it was all everyone could talk about lately.

Ella and Jesse were going together. And of course, so were Tori and Noah plus Harper and Emerson.

Technically, Rey was going solo no matter how much we all insisted we could set her up with someone.

Although, to be fair, she had reason to avoid me setting her up with someone, after last year's incident...

I had a feeling she already had her heart set on someone else, anyway.

But it was okay because we were all going together as a group. Rey and I could definitely hang out. Technically, if things kept going the way they were, I'd be there as Ian's date, but at the end of the day, I knew we were just friends. So I didn't want to spend all night attached to him at the hip.

I wanted to catch my breath a little after everything that had happened the past few weeks.

I never expected for things to turn out this way, and I wanted to make sure that I didn't make the mistake of believing any of it was real.

Bethany would be there too, and I wondered if that's when Ian would really try to get her back. In fact, my money was on him getting her back in time to take her to Homecoming.

Not me.

We hadn't really talked about Homecoming yet so I knew I couldn't assume we were going together.

Which meant there was a good chance he'd break

up with me this week. Our fake relationship had everyone convinced it was real, but I knew the goal of this thing was to get her back.

If he broke up with me within the next few days, then I knew that he still loved her. Or that he was finally ready to move on.

As crazy as this ride had been, it'd be weird to have it come to an end, but I knew it had to.

But that was okay because we'd still be friends.

We wouldn't be napping on each other's shoulders on the bus or feeding each other gummy worms or sharing a blanket, but I'd still have Ian.

And that's what mattered.

At least that's what I told myself.

Lunch time came, but Ian wasn't in our usual meeting spot at my locker.

He usually met me here, but today he was nowhere to be found. Not in the halls and not in the lunch line when I got there.

I could have texted him, but I reminded myself it was no big deal.

My phone buzzed, and I saw it was a text.

But it was just Harper.

Harper: Coming? :)

I texted her back, letting her know I was on my way.

My thoughts went back to Ian.

Maybe he was already patching things up with Bethany. Word was that things with her new boyfriend weren't going as well as she had hoped.

I scanned the cafeteria one more time. No Ian.

And no Bethany. She was usually already in the cafeteria, although she always pretended we didn't exist.

I sighed and grabbed my lunch. Found my seat at the #BFFs table.

"Where's Ian?" Tori asked. She seemed a little odd, but I couldn't read why.

I shrugged. "Not sure."

Harper and Ella exchanged glances, and I blurted out, "What?"

"Uh, nothing," Ella said. "How's your day going so far?"

But her question made it seem like they knew something I didn't.

I exhaled and looked at every one of them in turn. "If you guys know something, you can just spit it out. I can handle—"

Just as I wondered inside if I could handle Ian somehow letting me down, I heard a loud commotion behind me.

I turned to find Ian practically leading a parade of guys toward me.

He had a large poster in hand, but all I could see was the back. It had to be the back because there wasn't anything on it.

What was going on? Whatever it was, it had Chris all riled up, jumping up and down and whooping. Several of the guys pushed Ian toward our table.

He grinned sheepishly but would hardly look my way.

I glanced back at the girls, and they all had knowing expressions on their faces.

Harper looked like she couldn't smile big enough.

I turned back to Ian, who now stood just a few feet away.

Chris produced a microphone from out of nowhere and switched it on before holding it in front of Ian.

Several people already had their phones out, and I shook my head. This could not be happening.

But I bit my lip to keep my smile from spreading wide.

Ian turned his poster over and spoke, his voice trembling just a bit before gaining confidence with each word. I glanced at the poster, hearing the same words he had obviously carefully drawn out and colored in.

A soccer ball took the place of every single O in his question.

My eyes went back to him.

He hardly contained his smile. "Lena, I hope I'm not being too forward, but can I score a date to Homecoming with you?"

ELEVEN

Was this happening?

Was this real, or was I dreaming?

The entire cafeteria waited with bated breath for me to give an answer, but I only had the eyes for Ian.

My brain tried to figure out what all of this meant, but I realized I couldn't think about that now. Ian needed an answer.

I stood up and nodded. "Yes, I'll go to Homecoming with you."

The cafeteria exploded in cheers and claps.

Chris jumped about three feet into the air, and I wondered for a second why he had never tried out for basketball.

Ian handed his poster off to one of the guys and then came in for a hug.

I wrapped my arms around him too. I swore it felt like winning a championship. The adrenaline, the cheers and screams.

Except this felt even better.

I laughed as we pulled away. Ian stayed close, though. I took him in. "I can't believe you did this. You are the cheesiest…sweetest boyfriend ever."

Ian glanced down and then back at me. "I hoped you would like it. And I'm kind of relieved you said yes. Otherwise, that would have been pretty embarrassing."

I smiled. "How could I not say yes?" Especially when it came to Ian. "I told you before I'd go with you."

But for some reason, this—what had happened today—felt different.

Then, without thinking too much about it, I kissed him.

In front of everyone.

I couldn't hold it in any longer.

My lips brushed his, and it felt like breathing in rich oxygen after a long sprint. It brought me back to life.

I pulled away, only to hear even more whoops and cheers.

Searching Ian's face for a reaction, I ignored all of it and just focused on him. But he wasn't looking at me anymore.

"Okay, okay, back to your seats," Mr. Nguyen said. He broke up the circle of guys, and everyone finally walked back to their tables, still excited. "I should have been a physician," he muttered on his way back to the teacher's table.

Ian said, "See you at practice?"

I nodded and waited for that forehead kiss which

had become our norm. But it didn't come. Instead, he followed Chris and the rest of the guys back to their usual table without a second look back.

I took a seat, suddenly second-guessing everything that had just happened.

Ella, Harper, Rey, and Tori congratulated me and immediately started talking about how that was the cutest thing they'd ever seen, but all I could do was nod and give them the best smile I could muster.

I had kissed Ian for real.

But had it been the right thing to do?

———

IAN'S HAND gently touched my elbow just before I entered the girls' locker room.

"Hey," he said quietly.

Practice had been intense, and everyone was eager to leave, including me.

Especially since Ian had hardly looked at me the entire time.

Now he stood in front of me, his jaw set and his hands clasping his goalie gloves as he glanced anywhere but at me.

"What is it?" I asked, realizing I actually felt nervous.

It only made sense. I had kissed him, maybe for real, in front of everyone earlier.

Instead of kicking a soccer ball, I just wanted to kick myself.

Ian exhaled slowly, like he was wondering just how

to word what he was about to say. "Lena, I, uh—what happened earlier," he tried, still mostly staring down at his cleats.

I wanted to say so many things, ask him if it had been the wrong thing to do. Say sorry. Say I wasn't sorry. But I bit my lip and let him finish.

I had to know what Ian thought first.

He looked at me for half a second. "I don't think we should kiss on the mouth," he finally said.

Oh.

My stomach fell, and suddenly, I felt so stupid, like the world's biggest idiot.

I opened my mouth to find something to say, some combination of words that would make this go away, make the feeling of wanting to throw up disappear, but Ian beat me to it.

He swept his hand through his hair. "It's not you. It's just…We both know this…isn't real."

Just like that, something inside me cracked, but somehow I kept my focus on Ian. "Right," I uttered.

"I don't want to take advantage of you, Lena. You're special. Whoever you decide to kiss, it should mean something. You agreed to do this for me, to make everyone think you're my girlfriend, but I can't ask you to do that too. I'm already asking too much. Those kisses, Lena? Save them for someone special, okay? Not me."

He closed his mouth then, like he had already said too much.

I stared at him, studied him, the way his mouth turned slightly downward and the way his thick brows hooded his cool blue eyes. I swallowed and said, "I think you're right. I guess I just wanted to play along. I guess I got carried away." I hated the way my voice sounded. Tiny and unsure.

I hated it because it reflected just how I felt inside.

I regretted kissing Ian the second time. Letting an impulse get the best of me, but it wouldn't happen again.

Maybe for a moment, I'd forgotten that this whole thing was fake. A show put on by us for Bethany. But that's all it was.

A couple of the guys walked out of the locker room, froze when they saw us, and pretended not to see us. They kept walking.

Ian gave them a small wave and turned to me. "So, uh, I'll see you at tomorrow's game?" he asked.

I nodded. "Yeah. See you there."

Then I shoved my hands into the pocket of my hoodie and headed toward the locker room, wishing for the first time ever I could take a kiss back.

———

THE NEXT DAY, Coach came up to me after our game. A game I had not done my best in.

Katie and Samantha looked my way, and I quickly pretended I hadn't seen them, that I was looking somewhere else.

"Lena? Did you hear me?" Coach asked.

I nodded, but then I realized he was waiting for an answer. What had he said?

"I said, are you okay?" he tried again. He was older like my dad. Except, unlike my dad, he didn't have a problem with yelling during an entire game.

There had been lots of yelling tonight, especially when I'd missed an incredibly easy goal.

Just thinking about it made me want to kick something. "I'm fine," I said. "I'm just not feeling a hundred percent." I coughed, then, hoping he'd let it go.

He sighed, patted me on the shoulder, and said, "Okay, then. Get some rest. I hope you're not coming down with the flu."

I shook my head. "It's just a headache."

Maybe I had finally convinced him because Coach finally left, his clipboard in hand.

How had I missed that goal?

The opposing team had lost half their games this season, and we'd just barely beat them. No thanks to me.

I was just glad my dad hadn't been able to make it. Seeing the disappointment on his face would have just made it worse.

When I got to the locker room, the rest of the team's chatter about some party obviously quieted down. I didn't say a word, just changed so I could get out of there.

They knew something was off with me, but I did not want to stick around and talk about it.

When I got to my car, my phone buzzed with a text. It was from Ian. This was the first time we had talked since yesterday's mortifying conversation outside the locker room.

Ian: Hey

Gotta love the one-word text.

Lena: Hey

Those three little dots popped up for what seemed like forever.

Was he writing his life story or something? Typing out two words?

I drummed my fingers on the console beside me, ready to go home. But I had to see Ian's message first.

Finally, it came in.

Ian: Want to go to Chris's party?

I stared out the windshield, wondering just how I felt about that.

Not sure I wanted to be around Ian right now.

I began typing out a text, letting him know I was tired and just wanted to go to bed.

But before I could finish, another text from him came in.

Ian: Listen, sorry about yesterday. It wasn't your fault. This was all my idea. I just don't want to lose you. You know you're like my best friend. And I thought it would be fun if we went to Homecoming together, but it doesn't have to be a big deal if that's not what you want.

I read his message over and over again. Each time it softened the exterior of my heart until it crumbled, leaving only the huge soft spot I had for Ian. Even if reading that I was his best friend made me feel both awesome and a little…something.

Lena: Fine… You're my best friend too. You know, that isn't a girl. Pick me up in an hour?

I turned on my car, shivering from the cold air but warm inside from Ian's message.

My phone buzzed again, and I picked it up right away.

Ian: You got it ;)

TWELVE

Chris's party wasn't like his last party, mostly the soccer teams and a few other people.

Apparently, Chris had gone all out and invited just about everybody in our school.

As soon as Ian and I walked in, I wondered if we should even stay. I was all for having a good time, usually, but not if that meant doing something stupid like drinking.

No, thanks.

A couple guys passed us, each carrying a red solo cup. "Maybe we should do something else. Bowling or something," I tried. I faced Ian.

He gave me an easy smile. "Let's just hang out for a few minutes. If it's bad news, we'll go. I promise. Besides, after the beating I took tonight, I'd rather lounge around on a couch listening to music than lunging a ten-pound ball at a bunch of pins," he said. "I'm worn out."

I observed the dark circles under his eyes. He did

look pretty tired. And the guys had had a pretty tough game. Lost by two, even after Ian had stopped several shots at his goal. "Okay," I replied.

I was starting to regret not hanging out with just the #BFFs instead. Tori and Harper were driving over from Ella's house to join me at this party, although now I was craving some girl time with them. It definitely beat the weird tension between Ian and me.

And being around dumb guys doing dumb things. Chris and the other guys were usually fine, but I recognized some of the guys in our grade. Guys who tended to get into fights or go too far with their pranks.

Bring things they weren't supposed to.

Ian brought me out of my thoughts and back to the party. "Want a drink?"

"Sure," I said and watched him saunter off.

I headed somewhere not filled with people. Tonight I was not in the mood to goof around and laugh. Not after the crummy game I'd played and the state of me and Ian.

I found a sliding back door leading to a back deck. It was quiet out there, and for once, I relished in the silence. Only a slight thud of music reached my ears, ever so faint.

Leaning against the deck, I exhaled and closed my eyes. It was cold, but I just pulled my jean jacket around me tighter.

I heard the door slide open behind me, and I turned, expecting to find Ian.

But it wasn't Ian.

It was Bethany.

I turned back around for a second, rolling my eyes. This could not be happening.

If I'd known Bethany would be at this party, no way would I have agreed to come with Ian.

Wait, had he known?

I tried to make sense of my jumbled thoughts, but Bethany came up to me.

She curled her lips into a close-lipped smile. "Lena, I didn't think I'd be seeing you here tonight."

Bethany's blonde hair reached past her shoulders. Her face was caked in make-up.

"Hey, Bethany," was all I managed through gritted teeth. I met her gaze head on.

It was like she sensed how tense I already was because she seemed to relax.

Wanting to get that smug look off her face, I made my voice light and loud and said, "How are things with the new boyfriend?"

Her smile faltered then, if just for a second. "Better, I'm sure, than you and Ian. At least that's what he tells me."

What?

But before I could ask her what she meant, she went on, taking a step closer. I held my ground as she talked. "I always knew there was something going on between you two. I'll be glad when this is over." She rotated her finger at me in a little circle, her other hand on her waist. "No way will Ian want anything to do with you when he's gotten you out of his system."

Blood rushed to my ears. My chest rose up and

down. "Like he would go back to you. I'm sure you'd love that, but it's not happening."

Bethany laughed. "I guess we'll see, won't we?" she said.

I felt like throwing up. Part of me said Bethany was all talk, just trying to make me upset. But another part of me wondered if she was right, especially after her comment about what Ian had supposedly told her.

The door slid open again, and I wasn't sure who to expect anymore.

But it was Tori, followed by Harper.

They came right over to me. Tori eyed Bethany, her face serious. "Everything okay?"

Bethany laughed again. "I was just leaving. Lena and I had some catching up to do."

Harper put her hand in mine.

Tori took a big step toward Bethany, who took a step back. "Yeah, I think you're right. You are leaving."

————

MY PHONE BUZZED.

Ian: Where are you?

Lena: Outside.

It wasn't long before Ian found me. He was lucky I hadn't just left without another word.

I just wanted to get out of there. Just be with my friends, more than anything.

Let this day end.

Ian walked toward me. Tori and Harper leaned against Tori's car several feet away. "What's going on?" he asked. "Are you okay?"

I scoffed. "Am I okay? Where'd you go? Getting drinks doesn't take twenty minutes!"

He blinked back at me. "I'm sorry, Lena. I didn't meant to," he began. "Some of the guys grabbed me, like literally picked me up and grabbed me, and wouldn't let me go until I played their stupid game."

His face, his voice, told me he was telling the truth, but I was still fuming.

"What happened?" he asked, coming in close. "Are you alright?"

I bit my lip then looked up at him. "Bethany happened."

Ian froze, didn't say anything.

"She told me you two still talk. Is that true?" I said, my eyes narrowing.

Ian glanced away. That's when I knew. "Just a couple times," he said, his voice hardly audible.

I couldn't believe this. "You have got to be kidding me," I said, laughing for some weird reason. "I'm pretending to be your happy girlfriend, and all this time, you've been talking to her." I began walking away, but then I spun around and looked at him again. I shook my head.

He tried to come in close, but I raised my hand. "Don't."

"Lena," he begged. "I promise nothing is going on. I wouldn't do that. You can't think that I would do that, do you?"

I met his gaze, and he waited for an answer.

I left without another word, hopping into Tori's car and wishing I'd never come to this party.

That I'd never agreed to this stupid dare.

———

TO MAKE MATTERS WORSE, it rained all day Saturday.

Not a light shower, where you could pull on a thick hoodie and go outside to kick the ball around without getting too wet.

No, it was the kind of rain that drenched you within a couple minutes.

The drops of water hit my window pane, and I sighed.

I couldn't even shoot the ball around the yard today to get my mind off of Ian and the party last night.

It was torture.

Maybe the #BFFs and I could hang out, watch a movie, or something.

Maybe even hit the mall together.

It beat staying home all day for sure.

I picked up my phone to text them, but then I saw a message from Ian.

I shook my head and breathed in through my nose.

I was *not* ready to talk to him.

But his words were right there.

Ian: Hey, I'm sorry again about last night. And whatever Bethany said to you. Can we talk about it, please?

Then another message.

Ian: I can't stand that you're mad at me. Let me fix this?

Ugh. How could a few words stringed together like that completely melt me?

Because they were written by Ian, that's why.

I groaned out loud and fell back on my bed.

What he did to me? It wasn't fair.

Opening his message, I typed out a message, thinking carefully about what I wanted to say.

Thinking because I did not like what had happened yesterday. Didn't like the pain, the hurt, during the argument with Ian. Or hearing Bethany and the smug sound of her voice.

There was a reason I'd only kissed boys for fun. I couldn't handle the drama. Even physical pain I could handle, the sprain of an ankle, a bad bruise on my thigh. But not this.

I liked keeping things fun. Easy.

Lena: I'm listening.

Three dots appeared on my screen, and I wondered just how Ian was going to fix this. The truth was I didn't like being mad at him, but I also wanted it to end. And not happen again.

Maybe it was time to end this dare once and for all. Then we could go back to what we had before. An awesome friendship. None of these complications.

As much as I would miss the cute and cheesy boyfriend/girlfriend stuff.

Ian: I think maybe the more time that goes on, the more I realize that maybe Bethany isn't right for me.

I read that message again, wondering exactly what he meant.

That he was getting over her? That he had feelings for someone else?

Gah. He couldn't have been more specific?

Ian: You mean a lot to me. Let me make it up to you?

I typed out a new message.

Lena: How?

Ian: Pick you up tonight? At 7?

Oh gosh.

Why did he need to pick me up?

Was this just going to make everything worse?

Part of me wanted to call this whole thing off right now.

But I couldn't bring myself to say it.

So instead, I said…

Lena: Okay.

THIRTEEN

A few minutes later, I made my way to the laundry room to dig around for my favorite jeans. It'd go perfect with my new shoulder cut-out top.

I saw Dad watching TV on the couch, realizing this was a good time to ask them if I could hang out with Ian.

By the sounds of banging pots and pans in the kitchen, my mom was nearby too. And it sounded like she was getting ready to make dinner.

She walked over. "Lena, oh good. I could use some help over here."

I gave her my best smile. "Actually, I was wondering if I could go out tonight?" I turned to Dad. He was the final decision maker around here.

His eyes left the TV and met mine. "*A donde y con quien?*" he asked gruffly in Spanish.

Maybe I hadn't thought this through. I could have just lied and said I wanted to hang out and eat dinner with the soccer team or with my friends, but I also hated lying to my dad. I sighed. "With Ian? Just to eat. Public places only. Promise."

I rocked back and forth on my tip toes, waiting for an answer.

My dad stood up, and I wondered why he felt the need to walk over. My mom's hands rested on her hips, her expression a little uneasy.

Suddenly, I felt cornered.

Dad sounded more serious than ever, which was saying something. "*Cuentame de este muchacho*," he said. "Is he your boyfriend, then?"

I held my hands behind my back. "Um, yeah," I said, realizing I should say it like I meant it, not like a question. "He is."

Dad grunted again, sitting down at the kitchen table.

That's when Mom stepped in. "And who is this *muchacho*, Lena? We don't know anything about him. We need to meet him."

"Mom," I groaned. "He's nice. Really. And you don't need to meet him."

I loved my parents, but sometimes they didn't understand that America wasn't like Mexico. Boyfriends weren't introduced until well after the first date.

It didn't help that he wasn't even really my boyfriend. If anything, Ian was just my boy friend. Big space in between those two words.

"I say we do," she repeated.

Dad grunted in agreement. "*Le dices que pase.*" He turned the volume up on the TV.

So that was settled then. Ian would have to come in and officially meet the parents.

If only he knew what he had gotten himself into.

———

AT SEVEN O'CLOCK SHARP, the doorbell rang.

I raced to the front door and opened it.

Ian stood there with what looked like a small box of chocolates in his hands. His eyes swept down, taking in my amazing outfit for a nanosecond before he recovered.

I smiled. "Well, hello there."

Ian didn't look so bad himself. He cleaned up nice. I'd been worried about overdressing for whatever this was, but Ian rocked a navy blue dress shirt and khakis that looked like they were made for his strong shoulders, thin torso, and long yet muscular legs.

He cleared his throat, and I remembered to move my eyes back to his face. He smiled, except it looked kind of like a grimace. "Uh, hi. You look great. I mean, uh, can I come in?" he said.

Giggling, I stepped aside. "You don't look too bad yourself."

He exhaled. "I did not think asking you out to dinner would mean needing to talk to your parents," he said quietly.

"Not regretting our decision to take me out, now are we?" I teased.

"Not at all," he said. For some reason, those three words had my stomach doing all kinds of aerobics inside me.

Meanwhile, Ian seemed nervous. In fact, I'd never seen him this nervous, not before or during any soccer game. "Sure. My parents are already waiting."

I led him to the couch. My parents sat at a right angle to us on the love seat. Ian immediately greeted them and shook my dad's hand, then my mom's, handing her the chocolates.

My dad mumbled back a response. My mom gave him her best English. Was it me, or did she look a little flustered? Probably the chocolates.

Ian sat down, and the interrogation began.

My eyes traveled back and forth between Ian and Dad.

Ian looked a little clammy, but he held his own, an anxious but genuine smile on the whole time.

Mom asked him about his parents (Lisa and Jared), what they did for a living (accountant and nurse), about where he was from (Georgia, but his great great grandparents had immigrated from Germany), and about a dozen other things.

Finally, I stepped in. "Dad, we need to get going or every place to eat is going to close."

Dad nodded and stood up. Ian did the same, and my mom and I followed suit. He held out his hand, and Ian took it. "Have her back by ten thirty."

That was all he said, but it was like he was communicating so much more.

Have my daughter back by ten thirty.

Don't hurt her.

I've got my eye on you.

I'm not sure I trust you.

Ian looked him dead in the eye. "Yes, sir."

Ten minutes later, we were on the road in Ian's car.

I glanced at him. His focus was on the road. Or maybe he was still recovering from the trauma he'd just gone through. "Are you okay? Sorry again about all that. My parents are really old-fashioned. Where we come from, just asking a girl out is practically like proposing."

He coughed, sputtering and pounding his chest. In about two seconds, the car ended up on the side of the road. Ian put it in park.

"Whoa," I said, holding on to the door. Ian gasped a little for air, and for some reason, I started laughing. "I'm so sorry. Are you okay?"

But he was laughing too. "Yeah, yeah. I'm fine. I just—that was intense back there. I wasn't sure I'd make it out alive."

We laughed for a full minute before Ian got back on the road.

I smiled, glad he was more relaxed. "So where are we going?"

We came to a stop light, and Ian met my gaze. "I know we're technically just friends and all, but then I thought…why not go on our first date?"

FOURTEEN

I'd never been on a date before, real or fake.

Suddenly, it felt like my life had become one of those romantic movies, the ones where the guys are completely unrealistically romantic along with the girl's always perfect make-up and hair. Even when she woke up.

When Ian led me into a nice restaurant, opening the door for me, my mouth literally dropped.

This was definitely not a place where you ordered a burger and curly fries. Drinks came in fancy glasses, not an obscenely large styrofoam cup with a straw.

I could have pinched myself. I'd never been in a place like this. But I also didn't dare seeing if this was real or a dream. What if it all went away?

Ian pushed in my chair for me and then sat across the table.

My eyes scanned the silverware, the multiple forks and spoons. "Okay, where did you learn to push in a girl's chair, and are you sure we should even be here?"

This place screamed $20 salad, and I did not want to have Ian go broke trying to make it up to me.

He grabbed his napkin, unfolded it, and put it on his lap.

I did the same, hoping I didn't look like a complete phony. My family definitely didn't go to the types of restaurants with cloth napkins.

He smiled. "My family comes here a couple times a year on special occasions. Sometimes my dad brings my mom on their date nights. It's their favorite."

I imagined a tiny five-year-old Ian being taught how to put a napkin on his lap and which fork to use when.

Definitely not something I'd been taught.

For my family, even a special occasion meant heading over to the local taco place, where you sat at a well-worn diner-style table with slightly ripped booths. But all of that didn't matter because the homemade salsa and *agua de horchata* were to die for. And we could talk and laugh as loudly as we wanted.

Dorothy, we weren't in Kansas anymore.

I glanced around, realizing I was the only person wearing jeans. "Um, Ian. Are you sure this is a good idea? I mean, we can go somewhere else."

Ian's voice was low and quiet. "You don't like it?" he asked.

I grimaced, not sure how to explain what I meant. "I guess I don't want you going broke buying me dinner?" I tried. "I just didn't expect to go somewhere super fancy."

He chuckled. "Don't worry. I didn't just bench-press weights over the summer. I also did some yard work for a few people. May as well spend some of it on someone. And as for this place being fancy, true. But their food is also pretty amazing. Way better than a burger and fries."

That had me grinning. "Okay, then." I picked up the menu beside me. "What should I try?"

Even with the fancy silverware and uptight waiter, dinner was great. The steak practically melted in my mouth.

More than that, it felt special. And the dessert we shared afterward—a thick slice of strawberry cheese-cake—perfectly topped off the entire experience.

I wondered if Ian had ever brought Bethany here. Or if I was the only girl he'd brought to such a special place. If so, what did that mean? Was he just being nice? Trying to make things up to me?

All burning questions I wanted to ask him right that second, but I also didn't want to spoil the evening with the mention of Bethany or what had happened between us.

After dinner, we still had time before I had to be back home but not enough to go watch a movie.

So Ian pulled into our local park. It was dark already so we couldn't take a walk.

I wondered if he just wanted to sit on one of the benches for a few minutes, watch the dying buzz of downtown not too far away. Luckily, it was only slightly chilly out. But warmer than it had been at practice all week.

Ian led me to the bench, and as we sat down, I couldn't help but shiver a little.

He shrugged off his jacket. "Here," he said.

I'm sure it was a meaningless thing for him to do, but it left me speechless. "Thanks," I managed.

His leg kind of touched mine, and I wondered if he noticed too.

But he seemed too focused on the sky.

I looked up with him. "What is it?" I asked.

Had his jaw always been so perfectly chiseled or had there been something in the cheesecake?

And why did he smell so good? I'd noticed his cologne a little before, but now, being this close to him, it was impossible to miss.

Ian turned to me, our faces just as close as when we sat together on the bus sometimes, listening to music together. But for some reason, this moment felt different.

Was it just me?

"This was always one of my favorite things to do growing up. Still is, I guess," he said, glancing back up at the stars.

"Yeah?" I asked with a smile.

His eyes stayed up there, scanning the twinkling blanket of darkness above us. All of a sudden, I felt tiny. Miniscule. Like I wanted to scoot in even closer to Ian.

"Have you ever been on a plane?" he asked, turning to me again.

I shook my head. "We travel to Mexico every

summer, but we always make it a road trip. Have you?"

He nodded. "A couple times. It's awesome, being that high, literally in the clouds and then above them."

I tried to picture what he meant, but of course, it was impossible. "It sounds really cool, even if I'm not sure about being squeezed in next to someone for hours."

"Unless you're just rich and can buy your own jet or something," he said with a small laugh.

I laughed too. "Now *that* I can get behind. First class all the way."

Ian pulled out his phone, putting his other arm around me. "Hey, you want to get a picture?"

And document this moment forever? "Uh, yeah," I replied happily.

I flashed my pearly whites wide while Ian went for more of a handsome grin. Goodness, was he becoming hotter by the minute, or was it just me?

He opened up the picture on his phone, turning it my way. "What do you think?"

"Perfect," I said. loving how cute we looked together.

"I think so too," he said. "Just what we need for Instagram."

Within a minute, it was posted and gaining likes, but as much as I loved that picture of us, all I could think about was whether he had posted it to keep up the charade that was our fake relationship or because the moment had been real.

And more importantly: which of the two was I hoping for?

———

IAN and I hung out more than ever. He picked me up in the mornings. We walked together to class. Went through the lunch line, talking the whole time. Then he'd drop me back off at home again.

It was weird seeing him all the time, hanging out with him constantly. It felt different than before.

And also, I found myself missing him during those times when he wasn't around.

On Friday, after another win for both the girls and boys and then a long celebratory dinner involving burgers and shakes, he drove me home.

But just as he pulled into my driveway and I reached for the door handle, his hand grabbed mine. "Wait," he said.

I glanced at our hands, and he let go.

"I actually wanted to ask you something," he said. We were both still in our sweaty uniforms. Ian's long-sleeved goalie shirt was covered in dirt and grass, and I was aching to take off my cleats and hop into the shower. But I wondered what was on his mind.

"What's up?" I asked, trying to guess.

It didn't help that he was taking his time.

"I already said I'd go to Homecoming with you," I teased.

He gave me a small smile before going back to

being nervous. "It's not that," he said. "My parents kind of want to meet you."

"Huh?" I said.

He shrugged. "My mom follows me on Instagram, and she saw the couple pictures I posted of us. And now she wants to meet you."

I blinked back at him. "Did you tell her I was your girlfriend?"

"Yeah," he said sheepishly. "I didn't think she'd like this whole fake relationship thing."

I nodded.

"I was also lucky enough to get the talk again, if you know what I mean," Ian said, blushing.

I was sure I was blushing too. "I'll let her know she has nothing to worry about," I teased. "But yeah, sure. I guess I can come over sometime."

Ian grimaced. "She…kind of already planned a dinner for tomorrow. She says it's not a big deal, but it kind of is so I guess wear what you'd wear to church?" he tried.

I sighed. "Got it. Cool. Dress conservative." Then I opened the car door. "Oh, and Ian?"

"Yeah?" he asked.

"You owe me. You owe me big time." I winked at him.

He scoffed. "Whatever. After what I went through with your dad, this is nothing!"

All of a sudden, a huge question came to mind, and no matter how much I didn't want to mention Bethany, I had to ask it. "Um, can I ask you something?" I said.

He nodded. "Anything."

I exhaled, wondering if that was actually true. "This dare, like, what we're doing? Are you sure it's not time to end it? I mean, if you're over Bethany, what's the point?" There was an awkward pause. "And if you're not, then…I'm sure it's not too late to get her back…" My voice faded until it was nothing.

Ian stared into my eyes for what felt like forever. His hand reached for my cheek, grazed it ever so slightly. "What if I just want to keep doing this?"

Mostly surprised I hadn't passed out hearing him say that, I met his eyes.

His question, the tone of his voice, sounded like a dare.

One I definitely wanted to take.

FIFTEEN

Now I knew what Ian had felt like being interrogated by my parents.

Just like Ian, I was more nervous than any soccer game I'd ever played, even when we'd played against the toughest teams.

I linked my arm with Ian's and walked to the front door of his house, hoping his mom and dad liked me and that I made a good impression.

Before we could even knock or touch the doorknob, the door swung open.

A boy and girl stood there, nicely dressed but with clearly mischievous grins on their faces. They looked pretty close in age. "Mom, Ian's girlfriend is here!" the girl yelled. She had a bow in her hair the size of her head, kind of like the ones Tori wore with her cheer uniform.

I glanced at Ian.

"Sorry," he said. "Lena, this is Jacob and Mia. And you two," he said, pointing at them, "settle down or I'll sit on you."

They took off giggling. I saw another younger brother on the couch, but this one looked old enough to stay on his best behavior.

Or at least play video games instead of running around non-stop.

A middle-aged woman stepped toward us from the kitchen. "Hi! You must be Lena." She was all smiles, and I relaxed just a little.

I stuck out my hand, but she came in for a hug. "Hi," I said, awkwardly, not expecting all the contact. But hey, it beat the disapproving glare I was expecting. It wouldn't be my first one.

Especially since teachers often labeled me the "loud one."

"Hi, Mrs. Reynolds. It's a pleasure to meet you," I said with my best smile.

She smiled back, and I relaxed just a little. "Pleasure to meet you, Lena. I told Ian here that I just had to have the gorgeous girl I saw in his Instagram picture over for dinner."

Ian shook his head, clearly embarrassed. "Maybe we should head into the dining room. Need any help carrying anything in there, Mom?"

But he was already on his way over to the kitchen. "Yes, sweetie! The two containers on the counter, please."

Mrs. Reynolds led me to the dining room, where Ian's dad was waiting.

After more awkward introductions, getting Ian's three siblings to join us, and blessing the food, we began to eat.

I counted down the minutes until I could go home, hardly able to stay still. I was itching to run, feel the cool air on my skin, and kick my soccer ball back at home. But at this rate, it would definitely be dark by the time Ian dropped me off.

And the stilted conversation came to an end.

After dinner, though, the kids clamored to go outside to play.

Mrs. Reynolds hesitated, but thankfully, her husband spoke up first. "Actually, maybe a walk would do everyone good."

I could have jumped up and down. "I agree. Nothing like fresh air, don't you think?"

Ian's siblings headed straight for the yard, though. I glanced at the jump rope in his sister's hands. Not to mention the soccer ball across the yard. "Why don't we hang out with the kids?" I asked Ian, hoping he'd get the hint that I'd rather do that than go through more small talk with the adults.

He shrugged. "Okay, sure. But you can play with Amy. She's tireless, that one."

Within minutes, I was teaching Amy how to double dutch.

"Ian, your girlfriend is cool!" she said, which made me laugh out loud.

Ian's parents watched us from their fold-up chairs, drinks in hand and smiles on their faces.

Ian was busy playing soccer with his brothers, and I wanted to join. "Come on," I told Amy. "Let's go play with them."

But she didn't look so excited about that idea. "I don't know. They always knock me down. I'm no good."

I put my hands on her shoulders, leaning down towards her. "Don't worry. You can be on my team."

By the time the sun went down, sweat dripped down my forehead and back, and I realized maybe I shouldn't have taken our game so seriously.

The curls in my hair had completely fallen out, and instead of looking romantic, my hair now looked like a rat's nest. Oops.

I walked over to Ian and hoped the setting sun kept his parents from realizing what had happened to my hair. "Maybe I should head home now. I don't want your parents to see me like this inside your fully lighted living room. And for the hooligan I obviously really am," I added.

He chuckled. "I think you look great. And for the record, everyone loves you." Ian stopped then, like something had occurred to him just then.

Then I realized why. I distinctly remembered him saying a while back that his mom had not liked Bethany.

So hearing that his family already liked me?

I was on top of the world.

———

"SO WHAT TIME do you have to be back home?" I asked Ian.

He glanced at me for a quick second before

getting his eyes back on the road. "Before eleven. Plenty of time to get some frozen yogurt."

"Are you sure?" I asked him. "I thought you were going to take me home?"

He glanced at me again. "Well, you said you wanted to change and get the dead leaves out of your hair."

"True. I'd also like to get out of this dress and back into my jeans. But I also definitely could go for some frozen yogurt. All that running made me hungry," I said.

Ian grinned. "Me too. By the way, you and Amy only won because you cheated. Tickling opponents is definitely a red card in my book."

I laughed, remembering how hard his brothers had been laughing, lying there on the grass while I tickled them endlessly and Amy made a goal. "That was fun."

Ian went on. "And tripping me so she could get a clear shot? Also not cool." But he was smiling as wide as me.

After I ran inside my house, brushed the tangles out of my hair, slipped into some jeans, and called to my parents that I'd be back later, we left in search of frozen yogurt.

Ian pulled his car into the frozen yogurt shop in no time. We loaded our favorite flavors with about a dozen toppings and found a solitary table in the corner to sit at.

I observed his cup and what clearly looked like

gummy worms and chocolate syrup. "That looks gross," I said.

He used his spoon to point at my concoction. "I can't even see your frozen yogurt!"

For some reason, that comment made me laugh until there were tears in my eyes. Ian began laughing too, which only fueled my laughter more. When I finally got my act together, there was Ian, grinning and biting the inside of his lip like he was trying really hard not to say something.

"What?" I said.

He stared down at his frozen yogurt for a second and shook his head. "Nothing." But then he looked up. "I just like the way you laugh."

Oh gosh. There were the butterflies. Why'd he have to go and say something like that??

Clearly, he felt the same way because he began eating his frozen yogurt without another look at me, and I did the same.

What was happening with us?

I could hardly focus on my frozen treat from thinking about it.

I wasn't sure if this weird tension between us lately was something that scared me in a good way or a bad way. Maybe both.

But I almost sighed in relief when Ian started talking again, and things felt mostly normal.

"I'm really glad you came over tonight," he said.

I licked some chocolate off my spoon. "Me too. Your family is a lot of fun."

"Nah," Ian replied. "You are. You make everything fun. Even riding a bus for two hours."

I smiled at his words. "I really missed us hanging out," I confessed.

He looked kind of confused. "What do you mean? We've been hanging out almost constantly since we started 'going out.'"

I played around with my spoon, pretending I was looking for more cookie dough pieces. "I just meant, since…you know."

Realization swept his face, and it almost looked like he'd tasted something bitter instead of sweet. "Oh. Yeah."

Hoping I hadn't spoiled the moment with my awkward comment, I said, "It just feels like old times is all. These past few weeks have been the best, despite accepting your stupid dare."

Ian chuckled, and things felt right again. He ate some more of his frozen yogurt, and I did the same.

When all our frozen yogurt was gone and our cups sat there empty, something like sadness spread from my chest to the rest of me.

Maybe it was the fact that all the cookie dough pieces were gone.

Or maybe it was the fact that I wished we could sit there forever.

Ian stood up, and I did the same, wondering if there was anywhere else we could go and hang out but knowing it was time to go home.

He took my cup and threw it away, and I breathed in deep, wanting to memorize this moment, this feeling inside me, forever. Something way better than the satisfaction of finishing a really tasty treat.

Ian came back, and I got ready to follow him to his car.

But then he outstretched his hand toward me. I glanced at it for a split second than up at him, trying to read those bright baby blue eyes.

I couldn't quite figure it out, but I took his hand anyway, trying to ignore the fact that my heart felt like it was about to leap out of my chest and focus on the perfect way that my hand fit in his.

SIXTEEN

E ven though I felt like I was walking on air for the next week, I had to buckle down and focus.

Our next game was a state qualifier. So no more ogling Ian during soccer practice. Coach demanded each and every player's best. More than our best, in fact.

"Just when you think you've used up everything you got in you, guess what?" he liked to shout during scrimmages. "You're only at 40%! You've still got 60% left in you! So let me see it!"

His motivational rants annoyed a lot of the other players, but it was usually the extra push I needed to do better than ever before.

And we'd need it during the game.

Our biggest opponent, Chestnut Mountain, was the team to beat at state. Last season, we'd tied against them at the state tournament. The year before that, we'd lost.

I definitely wanted to win state my senior year so we had to beat them. Had to.

Or else it would be that much harder to get a scout's interest.

And Ian? Ian was just as focused as me. Just another reason we clicked.

But before state and facing Chestnut Mountain once again, we had to beat this next team first. And then win two more games after that.

Game day came, and just like any other high-stakes game, time flew as soon as the shrill sound of the whistle reached my ears.

They made a goal, we made a goal, half time came and went, and then we were down to the last few minutes of the game.

Somebody had to win by the time the buzzer went off. We couldn't tie today.

And I wasn't ready to let the other team—and their super cocky forwards—advance to state instead of us.

But we couldn't keep the ball in our possession. Our defenders were struggling, getting tired.

I called to our midfielders to help them out, but they were wearing down too.

I screamed words of encouragement, pushed the girls to keep going, keep pressuring.

Then something crazy and awesome happened.

The varsity boys, done with their game and still high from victory, all stood up and began cheering for us. Stomping and clapping and chanting at the top of their lungs.

"LET'S GO, LADY EAGLES, LET'S GO." The deep boom of their voices filled the stadium, and my smile reached from ear to ear. Ian gave me a fist pump, and I waved, practically feeling my spirits lift despite how exhausted I was from running for the past hour and a half.

And their cheering worked. The entire team pressed a little harder. That's all it took. One of our opponents made a mistake, and then the ball was back in our possession.

Katie dribbled this way with the ball, dodging players from the other team. I made sure I was open and called to her. "I'm open!"

She passed. It was going too far...

I pushed my legs to carry me faster.

Got it! But a couple defenders were closing in on me. They were not going to let me shoot.

With my full focus on keeping the ball close, I relied on my hearing and peripheral vision to figure out what to do next.

Several feet away, Katie waved at me, shouted my name. I faked going this way then that, got a bit of space, and passed the ball back to her, far and long.

It was going to come down to this. There was only a minute left on the clock.

From the stands, the crowd went wild. Screaming at the other team to defend. Screaming at us to shoot. I ran forward toward the net.

Katie was going to shoot, but the goalie ran forward to grab the ball.

It was going to be a tough shot.

But then she glanced at me, tapped the ball toward me a split second before the goalie dove.

The goalie was on the ground. She realized her mistake too late. Yes! This was it!

I sprinted forward, met the ball, and kicked it, hard.

It sailed in. The goalie was fast. She dove for it again, but too late. It was in!

The crowd erupted in cheers and screams.

The referee blew the whistle. There were thirty seconds left on the clock. The other team still had time for another shot, but it was like our entire team had found their extra 60%.

No matter how hard the other team tried to get past our defense, they couldn't do it.

The buzzer went off for the last time, announcing the end for the game.

Katie ran over to me. Then Perry and Sam. We jumped and screamed and enveloped each other in a giant group hug.

Then the boys were there.

Lifting Katie and our goalie.

Cheering and screaming with us.

Ian found me, gave me a hug, and I decided this was officially the best moment of my life.

Boy, was I wrong. It was about to get even better.

He pulled away, but only so he could bring his face in close to mine.

"You did it. That play back there…incredible."

He squeezed my hands, and my heart continued to hammer. This time for a different reason.

Everything else, the sounds, faded away until it was just us.

Then he closed the distance between us, and I wondered if this entire thing was some amazing dream.

It couldn't be real, could it?

But the feel of his mouth on mine told me it was real.

It was the most real thing I'd ever felt.

I wrapped my arms around his neck, and his hands held onto my waist.

Whoops and cheers, louder than before, brought me back to reality.

We pulled away to find ourselves surrounded by both teams.

Katie clapped. Perry clasped her hands. Were those tears in her eyes?

I laughed. "What are you crying about?" I teased.

She pressed her lips together then said, "You guys are relationship goals."

I glanced at Ian, thinking about Perry's words.

Was that what we had now? A relationship?

———

IF I WAS WALKING on air before that game and bewildering kiss, now I had a permanent heart eyes emoji for a face.

I didn't want the night to end. Ever.

Ian's kiss had lit me up from the inside out, and all I wanted to do was kiss him again.

But before I could do that, Coach pulled me aside. "Lena, there's someone who wants to meet you," he said, clearly pleased.

We left everyone else on the field and walked toward an older looking man waiting near the bleachers.

He shook my hand, and I wondered who he was. Could he be...

Coach made an introduction. "Lena, this is Mr. Barry. He's a scout at the college level, represents several different schools. He'd like to talk to you about your future."

I beamed. "I'd love to talk about my future."

With that, Mr. Barry began talking about what a great addition I'd be to this school's team or that one. How he not only admired my ability to score while under incredible amounts of pressure but my ability to bring the team together.

I nodded like a dummy, trying to process his words and make sure I was hearing correctly.

Once again, WAS THIS A DREAM?

He went on, and I tried to keep my breathing steady. "I'd love to see you play again. Coach here tells me you're playing against Chestnut Mountain in a couple weeks. I'll be there, seeing what you can do. Needless to say, big opportunities await you, Lena, especially if you keep playing the way you do."

I nodded again, sure I looked like a bobblehead.

"Yes, sir. You can count on it, and I look forward to seeing you there."

My eye caught my dad standing not too far away. I waved him over and told Mr. Barry who he was. "He's helped me train since I could walk," I said.

Mr. Barry smiled and shook Dad's hand. "Nice to meet you. Your daughter is incredibly talented…"

The three of them began talking, and I slipped away, still in disbelief.

The girls waved me over, on their way back to the locker rooms. The stadium was starting to empty out, people making their way down the bleachers and toward the parking lot.

From a distance, I saw the other team walk with their gym bags in hand toward their locker rooms.

Katie high-fived me. "Ian was looking for you, but he went to go get his stuff."

I nodded. "We have to celebrate. That goal you made in the first half? It was epic."

We entered the locker room and changed into our warm-ups.

The whole time, I couldn't stop thinking about the game, that final goal, watching the boys cheer for us. Meeting Mr. Barry, the college scout.

And Ian.

Definitely Ian.

He'd kissed me. On the lips.

He was the one who'd made the rule about no more kissing on the mouth. How it wasn't right unless it meant something.

So our kiss...it had to mean something for him like it did for me, right?

Even though we'd technically kissed a couple times before, there had to be a different reason tonight's kiss felt like our first one.

And it was because it was 100% real.

SEVENTEEN

By the time we got back to school and stepped off the bus, it was super late.

But everyone was super hungry so we decided to meet up at the Shake Shack.

Ian drove us there, and the whole way, we couldn't stop talking about both teams' wins. All his saves. My game-winning goal.

And the whole time, his right hand squeezed mine while his left steered.

I was pretty sure the pulsing red hearts for eyes were back.

We pulled into the diner, and I stepped out, immediately shivering. I hadn't felt the cold before, but now I realized I hadn't brought a jacket.

I joined Ian, taking his hand again, and willed my body to stop shivering.

Ian turned to me. "Here," he said quietly, taking off his letterman jacket and putting it on me.

I slipped my arms inside and hugged the jacket

close. It was still warm, and it definitely smelled like him. "Good luck getting this back," I said.

He chuckled. "It looks better on you anyway."

I definitely could have debated that, especially with my post-game wild hair, but instead, we went inside.

We found everyone else and joined them. Together, both teams took up almost half the restaurant and several booths.

Everyone cheered when they saw us, and several of the girls definitely eyed Ian's jacket on me.

Katie nudged me playfully when I gave her a hug. "You two just get more adorable every time I see you, I swear."

Pretty soon, I was feeding Ian fries and laughing with everyone else.

As we sat there, I realized it didn't get much better than this. Laughing and hanging out after a game like tonight. One where we'd left everything on the field.

I couldn't believe this was my last soccer season in high school. Senior year. I just never wanted it to end. But I knew it would in just a few more months. All of us…we'd be in different places next year. A lot of us would no longer even live here.

It was a lot to think about, so I pushed those thoughts aside and focused on memorizing every sound, every laugh and smile, the heavy feel of Ian's jacket on me, his arm around me. The warmth of being so close to him. His voice, perfectly deep but kind.

I leaned my head against his shoulder and closed

my eyes, taking in a deep breath.

How was this real life right now?

It felt like a dream.

Ian spoke softly, making me open my eyes. His camera was right in front of us. "Say cheese," he said.

With my face oh so close to his, he snapped the picture then showed it to me.

"Perfect," I said. He was handsome as ever. And I looked...happy. More than words could say. "Send it to me?"

A few minutes (and my favorite filter) later, it was on Instagram.

I could hardly stop looking at us, and I wondered why I'd never seen him that way before.

I couldn't imagine us going back to being friends now. Not when being more simply felt right.

Several messages hit my phone at once. It was the #BFFs thread.

Tori: WHOA.

Ella: !!!

Rey: omgggg

Harper: Jumping up and down over here! Tell me this is what I think it is! :D

I practically squealed in my seat and texted them back like a maniac.

Lena: GUYS, I THINK THIS JUST BECAME REAL <3 PINCH ME

Lena: JUST KIDDING DON'T PINCH ME I DON'T WANT THIS TO END.

Then I sent about a million different relevant emojis.

So did they.

Ella: But how??? I thought you guys agreed this was all pretend…

Tori: I KNEW IT

Rey: TELL US EVERYTHING

Lena: I don't even know. I think it just happened. At the end of the game, we kissed. He KISSED me. And I know it was real. I think he feels it too.

Harper: What did he say???

Lena: I guess we haven't really talked about it, but it's like we don't have to, you know? Things are just…perfect right now. Like we don't need to say it out loud. I just can't even believe how amazing life is right now.

They sent even more emojis.

I put my phone down and went back to the conversation at hand, which involved a burping contest among some of the boys and most of the girls being grossed out. Thankfully, Ian had too much self-respect to participate.

I held on to him, eating my fries and still sure I had to be in some kind of dream.

We'd won the state qualifier at the last possible moment, a scout was pretty interested in me, my best guy friend and I had fallen in love, and I had the best girlfriends in the world.

Life was perfect. What else could I ask for?

———

LIFE WAS PERFECT.

Even if getting up at the crack of dawn wasn't. I

was actually pretty excited to get to school because it meant riding there with Ian.

Holding his hand as the morning sun's rays reached us through the windshield and warmed us up was everything.

We made it inside just before the warning bell. Ian checked the time on his phone. He only had a couple minutes to get to first period. "See you later?" he said.

I nodded.

He gave me a peck on the cheek. "Thanks. If I get one more tardy in this class…"

I gave his hand a squeeze. "Don't worry. I'm sure I can find my way."

Then he was gone, lost in the crowd of students rushing to make it to class on time.

By the end of second period, I was telling Rey all about our game on Friday. But most importantly, about Ian and me.

Rey doodled on her worksheet. "That is awesome. So you really think you've got a shot at playing soccer in college? I don't even know what I want to study."

"Coach thinks so. And I bet you'll find something. There's so much you could do, Rey. Writing. Art. Graphic design. Become one of those bloggers that hangs out on the beach all day or something, sipping a yummy drink with those mini umbrellas."

Rey glanced around awkwardly. "Yeah, I don't know if I could do that."

I scoffed. "You already write like all the time. All you have to do is post it online. I bet you'd get a million followers like that." I snapped.

She shrugged.

I gave her a smile. "You'll find something. Just watch." Then I gave her a wink. "I bet a cute guy is just around the corner too," I teased. "Or right in front of you. Just look at me and Ian. Who would have thought? Do you remember all of us a few years ago? Or in middle school? We were so goofy looking," I said with a laugh.

Rey nodded. "I used to have super long hair." She touched her super short hair. "And we'll be graduating and going to college soon." She frowned.

"What's wrong?" I said. "I can't wait to graduate."

"Well, duh," she said. "You already have a plan, and it's happening. Plus you're confident and friendly. You'll make friends wherever you go." That frown became a little bigger. "I'm really gonna miss you guys."

I put my hand on hers. "Rey, come on, you know we'll still hang out. Promise," I said. "And you'll make friends too and have a blast. I just know it."

She finally cracked a small smile. "Thanks. I hope so."

The bell rang, and we scrambled to finish the work we were supposed to be doing. Oops.

"The two of us together aren't always a very productive pair, are we?" I said, giggling.

She started giggling too.

We were the last ones to turn in our worksheet, the classroom empty by the time we picked up our backpacks to leave.

Rey and I walked into the hallway, zig-zagging our way to our lockers. Usually, Ian met up with me by now, but he wasn't anywhere to be seen.

I turned to Rey, who hugged her journal and textbook. "Want to walk together?"

She nodded. "At least until we have to diverge paths."

Diverge? Count on Rey to use the fancy language.

We linked arms and headed to our next class. A couple of hallways later, I waved bye to Rey and turned toward Math.

The bell rang just as I walked in, and I wondered about Ian. Maybe he'd gotten held up in class just like me.

I found my seat and took out my phone so I could text him. The teacher was at her desk, talking to someone, so I turned my back and tapped out a quick message.

Lena: <3 missed you!

I stuck my phone in my pocket, half expecting an immediate buzz but none came.

The teacher's voice cut through the loud chatter of the classroom. "Guys, work on your study guides for a few minutes! We'll get started in just a bit."

I dug through the sheaf of papers pocketed in my binder. Study guide, study guide, study guide…

Then a familiar name caught my attention.

"And I heard Bethany say she and Ian are finally getting back together. Can you believe it…" the loud whisper said.

I turned around in a flash, but it was hard to tell

who had said it when just about everyone was talking and laughing, hardly pretending to do any work.

Searching for the same voice one more time, I wondered if I had even heard correctly. Maybe I just thought I'd heard the names Bethany and Ian. Maybe...

Maybe my ears hadn't deceived me.

I turned back around, biting my lip, study guide forgotten.

Is that why I had hardly heard from Ian today? And the more I thought about it, why he'd seemed a little off this morning, like he wasn't quite hearing what I was saying? Like something else had been on his mind?

I breathed in deep, all those jumbling thoughts cramming into my mind and not letting me focus on anything else.

I hardly heard a word the teacher said during the next forty-five minutes before the bell rang.

But it couldn't be true... Ian wouldn't do that.

Would he? It had to be some weird rumor, started by Bethany of course.

That made sense. Because we were together now. Our kiss good night when he dropped me off at home after hanging out at the diner...that had been real. It had definitely felt real.

Everything from his jacket on me to the way he looked at me had been genuine.

So those whispers...they had to be lies.

Had to be.

EIGHTEEN

At lunch, I wanted nothing more than to disappear.

Ian finally showed up, but he was late and definitely not himself.

Maybe it was due to the rumor I'd heard earlier. The whispers had spread like wildfire from class to class.

I could have sworn the loud chaos of the cafeteria actually quieted down for a few seconds when we walked in.

Ian glanced around, shoved his hands in his pockets, and then attempted a smile, except his jaw was stiff.

I recognized that tic of his. Something was up.

"You hungry?" he asked. His voice came out strained, and for once, I wished I was anywhere but with him.

Or at least not in front of everyone in the cafeteria. It felt like a thousand pairs of eyes were watching us, seeing how we acted, maybe hoping for a fight. A loud break up, if they got lucky.

I hated this.

How had everything changed so fast?

Ian's voice broke through again. I remembered that he had asked a question. "I said, you hungry?" he tried again.

I shrugged. "Sure."

We didn't say another word the rest of the time in the lunch line, and the tension between us was excruciating.

Why didn't he just say something? Say it wasn't true?

Say it was.

I could have just asked him myself, but that didn't feel right either. The rumor was about him and Bethany so shouldn't he be the one to tell me what was going on?

The whole situation unsettled me.

Ian and I, we'd never even had an argument. Maybe a disagreement over which playlist to listen to or which play the other should have done on the field. But ever since we'd started this dare, we'd argued outside that party, and now it felt like a much more serious fight was brewing.

And we didn't usually keep things from each other. Not if they affected the other person anyway. If he needed to be told to suck it up and or stop doing that in soccer, I'd say it. And he would nod and say I was right.

And the same was true for me. He wasn't afraid to

tell me what I was afraid to admit myself. What I didn't even realize I was doing.

But now it felt like he was hiding something. Something that was going to blow our friendship—and our relationship—into smithereens.

Was that why he wasn't saying anything?

Had he gone back to Bethany?

Ugh, this whole thing was killing me.

I grabbed my tray and rushed off to my usual table. It wasn't until I was halfway there that I heard the lunch lady calling after me, letting me know I'd forgotten to pay.

This could not have become any more embarrassing.

Then Ian got her attention and handed over some bills.

I turned back around and finished racing to my usual table.

The #BFFs glanced back in the direction I'd come from. I kept my head down but when I looked back up, Ella's gaze followed someone across the lunch room. Ian, I assumed.

I sighed. "He didn't follow me, did he?" I asked.

Ella shook her head. "No, but he keeps looking over here."

Harper scooted closer. "Is everything okay?"

Tori put down her drink. "What's up with you two? I've been hearing all kinds of weird rumors."

I groaned. "So you heard them too? I was kind of hoping it was all just a figment of my overactive imagination." My voice trailed off. Definitely not my imagination.

Harper put her hand on mine. "I thought everything was great between you two, that—"

Tori interjected, "—you two were actually going out now?"

Rey nodded. "What happened?"

I shook my head. "I don't even know. Ian's been acting weird. Something is up. I'm just afraid to ask what," I said quietly.

Harper wrapped her arm around me. "You two will figure it out. I just know it."

Suddenly, tears filled my eyes. What if we didn't? "How do you know that?" I asked, trying really hard to keep my voice even.

Tori gave me a small smile. "We just know. You two are meant for each other. No way you guys have been such good friends this whole time, just for it to end like this."

Rey said, "I think the same thing. I can tell Ian is crazy about you. Maybe he messed up or something. But I know he'll fix it. You'll see."

Ella wrapped her other arm around me too. Then Tori and Rey scooted in on the other side of Ella and Harper too, reaching their arms until they made this almost kind of cool half cocoon around me.

In that moment, as much as it felt that my heart was starting to crack, I felt safe. But even so, I couldn't help but wonder if I had been completely wrong about Ian and me.

———

I SAW Ian at soccer practice, but instead of asking him about what I'd heard, I completely chickened out and decided to talk to him about it after practice.

I did need to give practice one hundred percent after all. Coach expected it.

And I also didn't want things to possibly implode in my face right before practice when we'd have to spend another hour and a half together.

Besides, I told myself, if something was up, he would have told me already, right? He'd had the chance to do so. Once, if not twice.

It was probably nothing anyway.

So I shoved all the doubt and worry from before and pretended that what was going on between us was no big deal.

Kind of like a big band-aid over a badly sprained ankle. But hey, it did the trick for a couple hours.

By the end of practice, though, the band-aid had definitely fallen off.

I gave the girls a half-hearted wave as they left the locker room, making sure I was the last one to leave. When Ian and I talked about this, we definitely didn't need an audience.

Exhaling big and slow, I finally made my way to Ian's car, really wishing I had driven myself to school today.

And that everything could just go back to the way it was the other night.

A lone figure stood at Ian's car, his back to me. I recognized his black long-sleeved shirt and his perfectly tousled post-practice hair. His neon goalie gloves lay on the hood of his car. As I approached Ian, my gym bag hanging from my shoulder, I noticed his head was down, and I wondered instantly what he was thinking about.

The last couple people other than us pulled out of the parking lot, calling out goodbye to us.

I waved to Chris, and behind him, Sam.

Then I went up to Ian.

Ian coughed and then said, "So should we get going then?"

I put my bag down. "I actually want to talk to you first." I could hardly meet his eyes.

"Oh," he said quietly. "Okay."

He grimaced, and my stomach sank.

Would I end up having to call my dad to pick me up after this conversation was over?

The thought of that made me want to throw up.

I took a deep breath and moved my foot around on the concrete like I had something to squash.

I stopped and looked up at Ian, making myself meet his gaze. "So, like, about today…"

Ian shifted uncomfortably. "About that, Lena—"

A surge of something like confidence or maybe anger or disappointment had me interrupting him. "Yeah, today," I said. "What was that about? I mean, I'm in class, and half the people are talking about you and Bethany." I fought the bile in my throat so I could finish. "Getting back together?"

He took a step closer, and I took one back. "Lena, just let me explain."

"Okay," I said, hands on my hips. "Explain. Why are all these rumors going around? Are they true?"

He paused, and I felt like throwing up.

"Ian, are they true? Have you been talking to Bethany? Because you said you were done with her."

He ran his hands through his hair, sighing out of frustration. "It's not like that. Yeah, I talked to her—"

"What?" I cried. "Why didn't you say anything?"

He spun around, resting his hands against his car and pushing his weight against it. "It's nothing!"

I scoffed. "Nothing? Really? Talking to your ex is nothing? Talking to the girl you're trying to get back—"

He turned back around. "It's no big deal. She texted mc, saying she wanted her stuff back so I took it to her house—"

I laughed then, out of sheer surprise. Or maybe non-surprise. Maybe part of me had been expecting this. Knowing it was all too good to be true. "What? Oh my gosh," I said, shaking my head. "I should have known—"

Ian came in close. "Lena—"

I took another step away from him. "You don't get it. Who cares about this stupid dare? I thought you were my *friend* before anything else. You could have just told me the truth so I'm not walking around like some…" I closed my eyes, exhaled, and looked at him again. "Just tell me one thing. Is the rumor true?"

He glanced away. That one moment of hesitation was all I needed.

I turned away then. Pulled out my phone and texted my dad to come pick me up at school as soon as possible.

"Lena, wait," he said, coming around so he could face me. He faltered.

I stared at him, my voice hardly above a whisper. "I can't believe you still can't see her for who she is. You deserve better."

"Lena, please," he said. "You don't get it—"

"Oh, I get it," I spat. "Just leave me alone." I began walking away.

He touched my arm, and I stopped. "Just let me explain."

His eyes pleaded with me, but inside, I was done.

I kept walking, wanting to put distance between us so he wouldn't see how much this hurt.

My dad texted me, letting me know he was just a few minutes away.

Ian called after me. "Things with me and her are complicated, okay?"

I spun around one last time. "Do what you want. I don't care."

Maybe I'd finally struck the right nerve because Ian didn't go after me.

By the time I got to the front of the school, my dad was pulling in. I got in his truck and slammed the door.

My dad glanced around, obviously not seeing Ian,

then his gaze settled on me. I faced the window, blinking back tears.

I knew Ian had to still be at his car, and I wondered if it was because he wanted to make sure I was long gone before he left too. That thought made me want to give up and just start bawling.

At least I could count on my dad to not pry.

As much as I loved my him, this was not something I wanted to talk about with anyone other than my friends.

And I guessed he didn't want to have that awkward conversation either because he didn't say a word.

NINETEEN

A few days later, things between me and Ian were not fixed.

And I was seriously doubting all the advice the #BFFs had given me at lunch.

To make things worse, it was game day.

Instead of being pumped for it, I spent the entire day distracted. Kind of sad. And definitely not with a champion mindset.

On game days, it was safe to say I usually even felt a little cocky. Confident. Ready to get on the field and kick some butt. Make some goals.

Today, all I wanted to do was crawl into bed, eat ice cream, and cry when Ross and Rachel broke up.

But no can do, I guess.

The entire girls' varsity team—and the coach— was counting on me.

So I faked a smile and got through the day, our uniforms on to encourage school spirit.

It was going to be a big game, and a huge accompanying turnout was expected.

Along with a sure victory so we could go on and play against Chestnut Mountain for the state championship.

We'd beaten this team once already this season. They were good. We were better.

But I hadn't been going through a rough patch with my fake-turned-real boyfriend then.

Why did life have to be so complicated??

Life had been sooo much easier when Ian and I had been best friends. Before a home game, I could count on his assortment of playlists to pump us up. We'd listen to song after song from the bleachers overlooking the field, nodding our heads to the beat and envisioning what an awesome game we were going to have.

But instead of looking for him after school so we could start our usual routine, I kept to myself, kicking the ball around in an empty baseball field. The baseball coach would pitch a fit if he saw me ruining the grass in my soccer cleats but whatever. I couldn't see Ian right now.

I kind of even wished that he would just go back to his easygoing, quiet yet goofy freshman self. But that was ninth grade.

We were seniors now. No going back.

The time for the game came, and we warmed up. Stretched together. I led the team as usual, willing my voice to be just as loud as any other day.

I told myself that I had to do this. I'd played so many great games this season. I could do it again.

Taking a deep breath, I walked out onto the field. Within seconds, the referee's whistle blew.

I pushed Ian away from my thoughts. I had to get this game over with and help my team win. The boys had their game afterward, and it was going to be a tough one. The girls had already decided to stay and cheer them on from the stands, but I had an excuse ready to go when our game was over.

The ball came toward me, rolling through the perfectly trimmed grass. I stopped it. Okay, so good so far.

Searched for someone to pass it to.

Found Katie. Kicked the ball hard toward her.

And watched it sail too far to the right.

No!

Three flubbed passes and one easy yet horribly missed goal later, I sat on the bench.

Coach looked at me and sighed, mumbled something about coaching teenage girls and went back to watching the game and yelling at the rest of the team.

We were down one goal, and if we didn't get our act together, we were going to lose, big time.

And by we, I meant me. I needed to get my act together.

During half time, I opened my locker and stuck my head inside, ignoring the pointed looks of everyone else on the team. Coach began his usual speech, going through us one by one and telling us what we needed to work on during the remaining half of the game.

He saved me for last. My head remained in the locker, my eyes closed. "And Lena?" I was sure everyone else was staring at me, wondering what the heck I was doing. "I'm not sure what's going on today, but the team is counting on you so get it together." His tone was firm but soft and I knew he meant well, but the words stung anyway. I hated that I was messing this game up for everyone.

Katie came over and put her hand on my shoulder. "Come on, girl. We need you, so get out there and make a goal or two, okay? Or get me the ball, I don't care. But it's like you forgot to put your batteries in this morning or something. Like you didn't drink your special Lena juice. Dig deep and kick some butt, okay?"

I nodded, but inside, I knew that the game was already over for me.

We got back on the field, but I just couldn't get my head on straight, no matter how hard I tried.

By the last five minutes of the game, I was holding back tears. I'd missed another goal. Not an easy miss like last time. It had been a tough shot, but nonetheless, I hung my head in shame.

If it weren't for Sam, our sweeper, and the tight defense she ran, we would have been slaughtered, but at least we kept the other team at bay. They didn't score again, but since we never scored at all, the final whistle blew and they won, cheering and screaming at the center of the field.

The rest of us walked off the field, silent and somber. I glanced at the stands just in time to see Mr. Barry making his way out. Had he seen the whole thing?

I shut my eyes, partly to pretend I hadn't just seen the recruiter and partly to hold back tears.

We joined coach in the locker room, and still upset with myself, I got ready to get yelled at for the next twenty minutes.

But what happened next was almost worse.

Coach stood in front of us, disappointment clear on his face. "A team is more than just one star player."

Ouch.

He went on. "I know it was a tough game tonight. Sometimes, one key player has a bad day and it throws everyone off. It happens. I get it. But I'm really proud of everyone for giving it their all anyway and not letting it completely derail you. That second half we just played was great. Not our best, not our usual, but you kept the other team from scoring again. Every single person gave extra effort today to keep the team working. Lena, I know you missed a couple goals. That's okay. You kept trying."

I nodded and sighed.

"I've seen exceptional players just give up and not care. I know you care. You stuck with it."

A few players murmured in agreement, and I wondered why everyone didn't completely hate me. Why I wasn't getting dirty looks.

Then Coach gave me the answer. "Normally, tonight's loss would mean losing our chance to go on to state. But thanks to our previous games and the points we accumulated, not to mention not getting killed tonight, we've scraped on by and will continue."

I blew out a breath. Thank goodness. Maybe I'd be able to sleep tonight without too much guilt weighing on me.

Coach told us to go home and get some rest. "We can't afford to lose our next game. We win that one, we get to go against Chestnut Mountain High School for the state championship. So I need everybody in tip top shape the rest of the season." He jotted down some notes on his clipboard. Then he muttered, "And not just physically either."

The girls got up and began grabbing their stuff, pulling on their warm-up hoodies and taking off shin guards.

I stood up too. "Sorry, you guys," I said. "It won't happen again. I promise."

Perry came over. "Don't worry about it. Happens to the best of us."

Then Katie came over. "But seriously, girl, go fix the boy troubles because we can't afford another loss. I really want that state trophy," she joked.

I bit my lip.

"We love you," she said, easing up. "But seriously, if anyone deserves that state title, it's us."

She was right. I gave her the best smile I could. "Count on it."

I had no idea if the "boy troubles" would be fixed by then, but I knew one thing.

I could not let my team down again.

No matter what happened, I wouldn't mess this up.

Coach came over, looking uneasy. "Lena, I'm not sure if you know this, but Mr. Barry was out there tonight. He came to see you play. I'm sorry to have to say this but... this might have been it. Tonight was your chance, and to be frank with you, I'm not sure there will be another one."

———

AS IF THINGS weren't bad enough, with my soccer career going downhill before it even really got started and the awkward state Ian and I were in, that weekend was Homecoming.

Great...

I'd been so looking forward to this before, and now I was absolutely dreading it.

I could have kicked myself.

Why had I agreed to this stupid dare?

Then another part of me was angry solely at myself. This was my fault. I should have kept my feelings in check, but things had gotten murky so fast.

I should have slowed down for a minute, figured things out, cleared up boundaries or whatever. But instead, I had just let myself get caught up in what was happening without stopping to think.

Ugh.

On the field, my speed was a good thing, but when it came to boys? Definitely not a good thing.

It had definitely backfired on me, and now I was

paying the price.

No more dares for me, and definitely not ones that involved boys…

Or friends that were boys.

What if things between us were ruined forever?

Homecoming was definitely ruined, and there wasn't much I could do about it. I wasn't about to text Ian and figure out if we were still going together. The assumed answer was no, especially if Bethany was set on getting him back.

Ugh. Let her have him.

As much as the thought of them back together made me want to curl up into a ball. I brushed away a tear.

No crying. I'd already decided I was to make the best out of tonight.

I had the rest of the #BFFs to hang out with.

And I was determined to have fun, even if it meant putting up with Ian and Bethany a few feet over.

They were not going to ruin Homecoming for me, even if the prospect of staying home with a bowl of ice cream and a good rom-com sounded way more appealing.

So the #BFFs and I met up at Tori's house and got ready together. Harper and I did everyone's hair and make-up, except for Rey, who did her own super emo but super cool look.

Just a few minutes before we were supposed to leave and meet up with the boys, we slipped into our dresses.

Mine was long and figure-hugging, made from a rose gold fabric that shimmered from a mile away. The sweetheart neckline showed off my lean shoulders and my hair fell down to my elbows in perfect waves, with a bit of it pinned on the right.

The matching shimmery eyeshadow, dangly earrings, and nude lipstick really completed the look. Along with my favorite set of heels.

But I could hardly smile back at myself in the mirror. I looked like a million dollars, but I felt empty inside, knowing I wouldn't have someone special to hold me tonight.

A certain someone special. Someone I'd be able to reach perfectly in these shoes. Shutting my eyes and taking a deep breath, I gave myself another reminder of the strict no tears policy tonight.

I promised I would have a good time tonight. With or without Ian. I needed this, especially after everything that had happened on the field recently.

This was senior year Homecoming, and nothing was going to ruin it.

And if life was anything like those cheesy movies on TV, then maybe tonight Ian and I would kiss and make up.

Maybe there was still a chance we'd end up on that dance floor together, swaying to a slow song with our arms around each other.

Maybe.

A girl could hope, right?

My heart gave a resounding no.

TWENTY

All through dinner with the boys, I couldn't help but stare at Ella and Jesse or Harper and Emerson or Tori and Noah and how stinkin' cute they all are.

The way Noah grabbed Tori's hand when she sat down or how Emerson looked at Harper. Or when Jesse put his arm around Ella after they were done eating.

I turned to Rey who was also flying solo tonight. "I guess we'll be each other's dates tonight, huh?" I teased.

She smiled. "Totally."

I pushed my plate away. If I ate any more fries, I'd be popping out of this dress later. "You know what that means, right?"

Rey blinked back at me, almost like she was a little afraid.

And for good reason.

"We get to dance together," I said with a wide

smile.

I definitely didn't plan on spending the entire night alone sitting somewhere watching everyone else having fun.

Rey looked like she wasn't sure about the whole idea, but she totally said, "Okay," anyway.

I gave her a side hug, loving her for saying she'd stick with me tonight.

Nothing like a good friend to help you get through a dateless Homecoming.

When we got to the dance, the first thing I did was search for Ian, wondering if he even decided to come tonight.

Was he like me, determined to have a good time? Or at home, watching mindless TV and pretending Homecoming didn't exist?

About twenty minutes in, I spotted him with a group of guys from the soccer team. Looked like he wasn't the only one on his own tonight.

I breathed a sigh of relief, and I realized it was because he was alone.

Bethany was nowhere in sight.

And it would be a great night if I didn't see her.

But, of course, that was too good to be true.

A few songs later, I almost ran into her in the bathroom.

Our gazes met for a split second, and then I left. No way was I going to give her another second of my attention.

I went back to the dance floor and continued dancing with Rey, whose sugar rush from the cookies and punch meant she could finally keep up with me. For the most part.

We jumped and screamed and moved our hips back and forth to the music. I shut my eyes, trying to forget the past couple weeks, the disappointment, the hurt, in both sports and love.

For a few minutes, it almost worked.

Then the song ended, and I opened my eyes, and it all came back.

I exhaled and turned to Rey. "I'm gonna go grab some more punch, okay?"

She nodded. "I need a break anyway. Talk about sugar crash."

She stumbled off to the bleachers to sit, pulling a journal out of her bag, and I went off in search of hydration.

I found the punch table, picked up a cup and the ladle, and began pouring.

After I took a few sips, I put the cup down and wiped the drops of sweat on my forehead with a napkin. Despite it still being pretty early, the dance was going strong, with hardly any room left on the floor. Turning to walk back to our spot on the bleachers, I thought maybe I could convince Rey to join me for another dance. If I could get the girl to put down her journal for a minute.

I pushed through the crowd, mostly couples, searching for Rey on the other side of the gym.

The entire place was dark, the flashing lights making it harder to find my friends.

Then my eyes landed on a familiar face. Ian,

dancing with someone. Her back was to me, but I recognized her red dress in an instant.

Bethany.

They moved back and forth just a few feet away, his hands around her waist.

The lights flashed again.

I tried to read the expression on his face, but it was too dark.

Then Bethany pushed up on her toes, reaching for him. I shook my head, refusing to believe what I was seeing. But how could I not, when it was happening right in front of me?

Meanwhile, the world went on spinning, people continued dancing, and the music kept playing.

Inside me, my heart broke into pieces. Worse than any soccer game I'd ever lost.

I turned away, knowing I had to get far away. Still searching for my friends in the crowd, I wondered if I should just go. Then Ian's gaze stopped on me. He took a step around Bethany and toward me. I took one back, stumbling into someone.

Then I ran.

———

I WASN'T sure what I would have done without the #BFFs.

After I texted an SOS to Rey, she found me in the parking lot, sitting on the sidewalk next to her car and hidden from view.

Maybe Ian had come after me. Maybe not. But I

did not want to see him right now. Not with mascara and the rest of my makeup streaming down my face.

Then Tori, Ella, and Harper were there too, leaning down next to me, and all I could think about was that thank goodness the boys weren't with them because they did not need to see me looking like a crying make-up monster.

They helped me into Rey's car.

Tori opened the back passenger door, Ella and Harper right behind her, to get in the back, and I shook my head, turning toward them. I wiped at my face with a tissue. "Guys, no, please. Go back in there and find your dates. I'll be fine."

Harper bit her lip.

Tori said softly, "You don't look fine."

Ella handed me another tissue. "We just want to make sure you're okay."

Harper nodded. "Let us go with you. We'll hang out. You'll feel better."

I shook my head and attempted to smile. "I feel better already. I just want to go home. Please, don't give up the rest of your night for me. I'll just feel worse."

Tori sighed. "I don't know…"

"Please, you guys," I said. "We can meet up later or something."

They looked at one another.

Rey spoke up from the driver's seat. "I'll stay with her, and we can meet up later at my house. Just text me."

I didn't love the idea of Rey giving up her Homecoming night either, but part of me was also glad she was.

Finally convinced, the rest of the #BFFs gave me one last hug and promised they'd be at Rey's house soon, armed with my favorite snacks.

The entire way home, quiet tears ran down my face and I stared out the window, wondering just how this night had turned into a disaster so quickly.

How could I have been so dumb? Obviously, Ian still had feelings for Bethany. I mean, what did I expect? For him to get over her, just like that?

Maybe that happened in the movies. Not in real life.

And it was my fault for thinking my life was a movie with the perfect happily ever after.

I wiped at the tears running down my face.

Life didn't work like that.

TWENTY-ONE

Homecoming was far from over when Rey and I left so I didn't expect the rest of the girls to show up anytime soon.

But that was okay. Rey and I went back to her house. Her mom took one look at us and said I was welcome as long as I wanted.

We went upstairs, and I slipped off my shoes and crawled into Rey's bed. She dragged her desk chair over to the bed and kept her hand on my shoulder the whole time.

She didn't have a TV in her room like I did, but I just wanted to lay there anyway.

Within a few minutes, there was a soft knock at the door.

"Come in," Rey called.

I turned around too, wiping at my eyes.

It was Rey's mom, a small tray in her hands. There were two cups of something still steaming plus some cookies and fruit. She set the tray down on Rey's desk and turned to us. "Just thought I'd bring you guys tea and a snack."

I sat up and wiped at my nose. "Thanks, Mrs. Hart."

She gave me a press-lipped smile. "Are you sure you're okay, hon?" She took a few steps toward us, her face etched with lines of worry.

I nodded. "I'll be okay. Thank you for the tea."

It was silent for a second, and she looked like she was deciding if she should ask me what was wrong.

Thankfully, Rey stepped in and said, "It's okay, Mom. Just guy stuff. Nothing serious, I promise."

Rey's mom didn't look totally convinced that she should leave us alone, but she did. "Okay," she said, turning to Rey, "Your father and I are off to bed, but wake me if you need anything, okay? Knock and let me know when the girls go home?"

Rey nodded, and she left, gently closing the door behind her.

I lay back down, pulling the covers up. "Your mom's nice."

Rey stood up. "You want something more comfortable to wear?"

A few minutes later, I was in a long night shirt. We both sat on her bed eating cookies and drinking tea.

Rey held her cup and reached for another cookie. "My mom says a warm drink always makes things better."

I smiled. "She's right." The hot liquid warmed me down to my toes, and I felt calmer than before. "My mom loves her teas too, but I never tried them before. This is actually pretty good, though."

I took another sip, my thoughts wandering back to that image of Bethany and Ian at the dance.

My heart breaking.

Even Coach's words to me. *Tonight was your chance, and to be frank with you, I'm not sure there will be another one."*

Tears flooded my eyes again, and I wished I could erase that both of those things from my mind.

Rey squeezed my hand. "Want to go downstairs and watch a movie?"

I nodded, needing the distraction, and we headed downstairs.

I insisted on a rom-com, but within minutes, my head was on her shoulder and I sniffled, the tears coming back and needing to let it all out.

Thankfully, Rey was the perfect listener. "I mean, it was one thing for us not to go to Homecoming together. But to end up with her? It's like he just didn't care about me at all, you know?"

Rey said, "Yeah," and I kept going.

"He wasn't just someone I ended up having feelings for. He was my best friend. But now it's like all of that is gone for good. I don't see how we could still be friends after all of this."

That's when the waterworks started again, at the thought of not hanging out with Ian anymore. And it wouldn't be easy because we had the rest of the soccer season to go.

Every time I saw him, pain would flash inside me.

And then I thought of graduation and going our separate ways, and that made me cry even more.

Rey had her arm around me, and she hugged me tight. "I'm really sorry, Lena. But I hope he'll at least talk to you about it and apologize. You never know. Maybe it'll work out."

I thought about that, supposing maybe there was a chance. Hoping there still was a chance but not seeing how. What I'd seen had been pretty clear.

And while the thought of losing Ian as a friend was what hurt the most, I wasn't sure I could get past this.

The both of us sat there, with Rey's arm around me. I wiped at my nose and my eyes, but the tears came anyway.

The sound of the front door opening and then voices broke the silence.

Two guys walked in, stopping at the sight of us.

The one with a pizza box in his hands said, "Oh, uh, sorry. We'll hang out at Wes's house instead." With a small wave, they were gone as quickly as they'd arrived.

"Sorry," Rey said. "That was my brother Hugo and his friend Wes. He lives next door," she finished quietly.

I sat up. "Is he…?"

She nodded, turning a faint shade of pink.

I smiled, glancing to where they'd just been a second before. "He's cute," I teased.

We went back to watching the movie, but before it

was halfway over, several soft knocks came at the door.

Rey checked who it was through the curtains, but sure enough, it was the #BFFs.

They were still in their dresses, but as promised, they'd brought tons of snacks to get us through our last-minute pity party.

Harper gave me a hug, then Tori and Ella.

We stood in a small circle, and I was glad more than ever that I had them. "How was the rest of Homecoming?" I asked casually but also wondering about Ian.

Harper took my hand. "It was okay. Not the same without you two."

Tori smiled. "What's a dance without Lena to out-dance everyone there?"

We giggled, and I knew it was true. That was something else that made me sad: missing out on all that dancing.

Harper became serious again. "Ian was looking for you, you know."

Tori crossed her arms, and I could tell she was not pro-Ian after what had happened tonight.

But Ella shrugged. "If it makes you feel any better, he and Bethany had some kind of argument and then he left. He seemed pretty upset."

Harper went on. "Like maybe he was sorry?"

I glanced at Tori. She shook her head a little. "He didn't have to kiss her."

The feelings from that moment, from seeing

Bethany and Ian kiss, came flooding back. So did the tears.

That was the thing about kissing someone for real. The risk of getting hurt was real too.

Why did I think it wouldn't happen to me?

———

AS FAR AS I was concerned, the entire dare was now off.

My friendship with Ian was probably done too. Along with my chances of being recruited.

Either way, I needed time away from him to think and let my heart mend.

Unfortunately, Ian was relentless.

It was the reason he'd gone from permanently stuck on the bench to one of the top goalies in the state.

I just wished he'd do what I was doing and give me the cold shoulder back for a few days until I could decide how I felt about him.

But when I walked toward my locker on Monday morning, he was already there.

Ignoring his messages all weekend hadn't been enough of a hint.

Or maybe it'd just pushed him to do this.

He shifted his weight, looking unsure of himself.

I stopped several feet away, debating if I should skip grabbing my books or do my best to ignore him while opening my locker and grabbing my stuff.

Then my mind went back to him kissing Bethany

the other night, and the tears were back. I clenched my jaw, willing the tears to stay put instead of spilling over. Shaking my head, I spun around to get away.

I'd barely made it around the corner when he was there, in front of me.

"Lena, just wait. Please. Let me explain." His eyes pleaded with me. His voice. I hated myself for missing his voice.

I hesitated for a split second, my gaze on the ground. Then… "No," I said, my voice sure.

When I went around him and kept going, Ian didn't follow me. I sighed in relief, wiping away a stray tear.

He didn't try talking to me again the rest of the day, not even at lunch, when we ran into each other as I was leaving the lunch line and he was walking into the cafeteria.

His eyes lingered on me, but he shoved his hands in his pockets and stayed where he was.

For once, I wasn't looking forward to soccer practice. Things were going to be so awkward with the rest of the guys and girls. I was not looking forward to the weird stares and probing questions.

When I walked into the locker room that afternoon, I was sure they all knew. News about Bethany and Ian at Homecoming had already spread through the school as had our run-in that morning.

Katie and the other girls gave me the same looks of pity I'd encountered the rest of the day. But I was glad when they kept the conversation on other things.

And when they didn't ask me why I wasn't chatting with them.

Practice couldn't end fast enough. Time slowed to a crawl, but finally, Coach blew his whistle for the last time.

When I walked out of the locker room, Ian was still there, in the parking lot. He leaned against his car, probably wanting to talk. I took one look at him and headed in the opposite direction to my car.

Part of me felt bad for him, wondering if I should just let him say what he wanted to say.

But we also had our next big game in just three days. That had to be my priority. Soccer was more important than ever, and I had totally cost us our last game.

It wouldn't happen again, definitely not because of a boy.

More importantly, I had no idea if I'd already wasted my chance at my dream, of seeing how far soccer could take me, but I was going to give it my all anyway.

Maybe after the season was over I could think about talking to Ian.

Or maybe not.

TWENTY-TWO

Maybe Ian finally got the hint because he left me alone.

Oddly enough, I missed him more than ever.

Normally, I'd be thinking solely about our game the next day, the one we had to win so we could go on to the state championship, but all I could think about was Ian and how our friendship had crumbled.

Talk about big bummer before the game.

But if I did as well as I had been doing at practice, at school, and at home, then I'd play my best game ever. I was counting on it.

During practice, I had channeled all my emotions into soccer, and it had paid off. My shots at the goal were better than ever before. Instead of thinking about Homecoming and Ian, I pushed my muscles to run even harder during sprints. The nods of approval from Coach and the cheers from the rest of the varsity soccer girls were a big motivator.

I'd also ignored the pointed looks the guys gave

me and Ian and instead envisioned myself scoring over and over at the game.

Plus I'd avoided Bethany like the plague, in the hallways and everywhere else. I was glad we didn't have any classes together, but that didn't stop her from appearing out of nowhere, evil smirk at the ready.

The final straw came when someone literally ran into me and I dropped my books. Of course, she happened to be walking down the hallway at the same exact time. At the sight of my stuff sprawled out everywhere, she laughed.

Glaring at her, I exhaled like an angry bull. Saying something really mean would have been nice, but I also hated the idea of getting in trouble and then benched the next day.

No way would I let Bethany ruin tomorrow's championship game. Or a second chance with that recruiter.

So I bent down to grab my things. Before I could pick up anything, though, Ian was there, my books in his hands.

He stood up and gave them to me, suddenly way too close. The smell of his cologne had me flashing back to our first date. My heart ached at the images of him picking me up, eating together at the restaurant, then sitting at the park together. And the perfect way he smiled...

Blinking quickly and pushing all of that away, I took my books from him, glancing at Bethany's now rigid face several feet away. She huffed and finally left, probably angry that Ian had hardly noticed her.

"Thanks," I muttered to Ian, my resentment toward him softening just a little.

He didn't leave, though, so I began thinking up an excuse to leave. Like getting to class on time. That would work.

I opened my mouth, but he beat me to the punch.

"Lena, I'm sorry, okay?" he said, his voice sincere as far as I could tell. "Really, I am. Can we just talk, please? I hate being like this with you."

I bit the inside of my lip, trying to keep it together. "I really don't want to talk right now," I said, still not meeting his eyes. Then I tried to walk away, but the touch of his hand on my arm made me freeze.

His voice pleaded. "Lena."

I finally looked at him, glad Bethany was gone. But a small crowd of people had gathered around us, with classmates seemingly at their lockers or talking but really just staring, waiting to see if there would be a make up or a blow up.

I wasn't quite sure myself which way things would go. But I didn't want to talk here, in front of everyone like we were some lame reality TV show. "Later, okay?"

Ian gave me a nod, lowering his voice. "Okay," he sighed. "Maybe before the game?"

No, not before the game, I wanted to say. The game was everything, and I didn't want to mess it up by having another fight with him.

But in that moment, all I wanted was to leave. For once, I didn't want the limelight on me, not because of this.

"Sure," I replied, turning and walking away before Ian could say anything else.

———

I HOPED Ian would just forget what I'd said about talking before the game, but I knew it wasn't likely.

After school, I sat by myself in one of the hall-ways, resting my back against a row of lockers and with a view of the soccer field not too far away. I had my earbuds in as I tried to get myself pumped up for the game, but I missed our playlist.

On their way to the soccer field, a couple of the girls on the team asked me if I was okay, but I reas-sured them that I was. "I'm just psyching myself up," I explained, pointing to my earbuds. "Like Michael Phelps." I made his legendary angry, pre-swim meet, meme-worthy face, and that seemed to convince them because they finally left me alone.

The truth was that I spent most of that hour trying not to think about Ian or look at Ian or remember the good times with Ian.

Thankfully, several texts from the #BFFs wishing me a great game finally distracted me away from everything Ian.

In the meantime, we had more downtime left before it was time to warm up. The other team was running late. Everyone else, the teachers and other students, had gone home for the day, but the game wouldn't start for a while. That's when Ian found me.

I caught sight of him down the hallway, and I immediately pulled out my earbuds.

He took several steps toward me, the sound of his shoes on the linoleum eerily the only sound for what felt like miles. "Coach was starting to think you were lost."

"Not lost," I said. "Just wanted to be alone."

I stood up, keeping my gaze on the science posters on the wall instead of on Ian. I began making my way down the hallway towards the double doors leading to the soccer field. Ian walked beside me without a word.

"It's weird, you know," he said, breaking the silence.

"What?" I said.

"You turning into a loner all of a sudden," he replied softly. "Usually, that's me."

I didn't know what to do but nod. I couldn't tell him I was a loner lately because it hurt too much to be close to him.

I knew we were broken, but I had no idea how to fix it, so the next best thing had been avoidance.

Ian sighed. "Lena, can we just talk, please? Maybe go back to where we were?"

Where we were? As friends? I wanted to ask. Or where we were after that?

I shrugged, stopping in front of a classroom. It was empty so I went inside, not bothering to get the lights. It was cloudy and gray outside, but it was more than enough light. Ian closed the door quietly behind us.

I leaned back against the teacher's desk and

sighed. "If you want to talk, that's fine, but we don't have a lot of time so we should make this quick."

He looked down, and I felt bad for a moment, wondering if he thought I didn't care about us. But then his jaw tightened, and he closed the distance between us.

He reached for my hand, brushed his thumb against it. I turned my head to the side, moving my hand away from his.

"I'm listening," I whispered.

He took a couple steps back, his hands back at his sides. "I'm sorry. About the dance—I promise, it's not what you think—"

I scoffed. "You mean you kissing Bethany? Dancing with her? I mean, it's fine if you're back together with her." I pushed back the flood of emotions that came with remembering that, not to mention everything I really wanted to say to Ian.

Just like that, the tears were back, waiting to spill down my cheeks, but I willed them to stay put. Go back. I did not want to cry in front of Ian.

I already felt like an idiot for being upset. Letting this happen.

Ian sighed. "I didn't go to Homecoming with her. And I'm not back together with her. She insisted on one dance. I should have said no."

I shook my head, that kiss on Homecoming night reminding me of how mad I was at him. Was it so hard for him to say no to her? Would his resolve always cave when it came to her? The rest of the horrible feelings from that night filled my chest again.

"I wish I'd never agreed to your stupid dare," I said, more to myself than anything else.

But as soon as it came out, I regretted saying the words out loud.

Ian was so quiet that I looked up at him. The hurt reflected clearly in his eyes. Guilt ate me up inside, realizing I wasn't the only one holding back tears anymore.

Great. "I just meant...it wasn't a good idea. Clearly, you're not over Bethany—"

"I told you," he said quietly. "I'm done with her."

"—and with us being close friends and all...I just should have said no." I stared at my hands. "I'm not saying this was your fault. It just..."

Never should have happened, I wanted to say. I should have remembered that it wasn't supposed to be real. But where would we be if I'd never take that dare? Friends? How much would we have missed out on?

It just made me so sad that it didn't work out between us.

"I get it," Ian replied. "You're right. I'm sorry for what happened at Homecoming. All I wanted was a dance with you, not her." I looked up at him, but he kept going. "But...that doesn't matter. Because clearly all of this is over."

I opened my mouth to ask him what he meant.

"I didn't realize this would cost us our friendship," he finished. "If I would have known..."

He stopped, and I put his words together in my

head, one by one. That's when the tears broke through the floodgates and streamed down my cheeks.

"What are you doing?" I asked, keeping my voice firm.

He stopped halfway to the door. Shrugged. "It's pretty clear that you don't want anything to do with me so no need to keep telling me to leave you alone. Or give me the cold shoulder."

Nausea rose in my throat.

"Bye, Lena," Ian said.

Then he was gone.

TWENTY-THREE

Tori shook her head and grimaced. We sat together in her living room. "That was a pretty crappy thing to happen right before your big game," she said. "I'm glad you guys won."

All I could do was nod and wipe away the tears that wouldn't stop. "I don't even know how I got through it. I just did my best to pretend nothing else existed, did my best to be there for the team. Oh, and Mr. Barry, the scout, wasn't there. Not sure if that's a good thing or not."

I explained what Coach had told me at the last game. Just one more thing that plagued me.

Despite everything, though, I'd gone out there yesterday and made a goal. Katie had made another one, and our defense had kept the other team at bay.

Meanwhile, I'd held back the flood of emotions around what had happened with Ian minutes before like a dam. One that had finally collapsed.

I didn't think things between us could get worse, but just like that they had.

"Apparently, we're not even friends anymore," I said. I could hardly finish the sentence before my chest heaved and I covered my ugly cry as much as I could.

Harper wrapped her arm around my shoulders. "Oh, Lena," she whispered.

Ella said, "Get it all out," and that only made me cry harder.

After several minutes, I wiped away the tears with my sleeve and sat up. Shook my head. "I should have just kept pretending. Why did we have to make things so complicated?"

Rey squeezed my hand. "How were you supposed to know that you'd end up falling for him?" she said. "Don't feel bad."

"Too late," I said with a forced smile.

"I bet he'll come around," Harper said. "You two said what was on your mind. It may take some time, but I'm sure he'll come around."

Did I want Ian to come around? He'd already broken my heart once, practically twice with our friendship and fake relationship breakup rolled into one. No way would I go after him and risk my heart one more time. "Maybe this is for the best," I said. "Friendships don't always work out. He'll go his way. I'll go mine."

That had me crying all over again. It was hard losing a guy I'd kissed for real and really felt something for. It was even harder to lose him as a friend too.

Tori handed me a tub of ice cream. "Here, girl. A little ice cream will make it go away…"

Harper and Ella stared at her. Rey stifled a laugh.

Tori gently took the ice cream back. "Okay, the ice cream won't make the bad stuff go away. But maybe we can watch a movie and have some snacks anyway."

We settled into the couch at Tori's house, the girls surrounding me and a warm blanket over my legs.

I could hardly focus on the movie. The bruise of my break up with Ian hurt a hundred times worse than a kick to the shin when I didn't have my shinguards on.

And it went so much deeper too.

———

EVENTUALLY, I had no choice but to go home, as much as I hated for my entire family to see that I was obviously upset.

My mom asked me if I was okay about a hundred times before dinner was even served. She didn't even make me help her make it.

My sister Maria wouldn't stop staring at me, and my dad was more quiet than ever at the dinner table, hardly even looking at me.

I just wanted to go to bed. "Can I go? I have lots of homework, and I'm tired," I said, setting my fork down.

My mom glanced at my full plate of food then said, "Lena, you've got to eat something. You can't let yourself whither away—"

"Even if it's because of a boy," Maria interjected matter-of-factly.

I rolled my eyes, even though my parents hated when I did that.

"*Dejala ir*," my dad said quietly, and I almost fell over in relief.

I got up, left my plate by the sink, and practically ran to my room. Shutting the door behind me, I sighed and made it to my bed.

Maybe I could talk to my friends.

Sure enough, Harper told me about her latest adventure with Emerson at the nursing home they still volunteered at. Ms. Ellie had just gotten back from her trip with her daughter to Belize, and she had the tan and hilarious stories to prove it.

That made me smile.

A soft knock at my door interrupted my text message back to the #BFFs, asking just what kind of stories Ms. Ellie had shared with Harper.

I sat up and turned on my lamp, realizing I'd been in the complete dark. "Yeah?" I said. Maybe it was Maria, wondering what I was so upset about and wanting to satisfy her curiosity. Or Mom with a pile of folded laundry for me to put away.

Instead, my dad popped his head in then came in, looking really uneasy.

Whoa.

He never came in here. After dinner meant moving to the couch for some TV.

But there he was. He sauntered a few steps in, brushing a hand through his hair and looking around nervously. His fingers were thick, easily twice the size of mine. When I was little, I would put my palm up against his large one, wondering when I'd grow big enough to catch up to his size.

Dad took a seat on the edge of my bed. Was this about my last game? Was he making sure I did my best at tomorrow's big game against Chestnut Mountain? Remind how important it was to win the state championship? Give me some last minute pointers?

The silence between us was deafening. I waited for him to say something.

Finally, he opened his mouth, his gaze still anywhere but on me. "Selena," he began in Spanish, his body language awkward and his voice hardly above a whisper. "I don't know what's going on. Maybe trouble at school with your friends or that boy. I know this age is hard. I remember," he went on in Spanish.

More silence.

Was he remembering what being a teenager had been like? His childhood hadn't been anything like mine. He'd grown up in Tijuana, Mexico. Hardly gone to school. Had to work from an early age.

He went on in Spanish. "I know maybe it's not something you want to tell your parents about. I understand. This is the age where you start to figure things out for yourself, make your own choices." He sighed and nodded, glancing at me.

I nodded too, not sure what to say, if I was supposed to say anything.

"We've raised you right. I know you make good choices so we trust you, Selena."

Another pause, and I wondered if my dad would go mute for a year after this. When it came to talking, I could probably go on forever, but my dad seemed to have a limit. He even sounded exhausted. Or maybe it was his age.

"I just want you to know that sometimes life is going to be really hard, *mija*. It's going to throw many things your way. Good and bad. Only you can decide how you will deal with it. What kind of person you will become. But remember that you are strong. I've seen it on the field. And I know it's true off the field too."

He looked like he might say something else, but then he didn't. Instead, he exhaled, as if everything he'd just said had been a Herculean effort.

Then he stood up, patted my shoulder, and began to leave.

I got up. "Dad, wait," I said in Spanish.

He turned around, and I wrapped my arms around him. It had been forever since I'd done this because we rarely hugged, but I wanted him to know that I was glad he cared. "*Gracias, papá*," I said.

He nodded one more time and closed my bedroom door quietly behind him. Hardly making a sound.

I sighed and went back to bed, my spirits lifted. He wasn't worried about tomorrow's game. And neither was I.

As hard as it would be to focus on the game and ignore my broken heart, I knew I could do it.

For me and for my dad.

TWENTY-FOUR

That night, I lay in bed, staring up at the ceiling and wishing I was asleep.

I had a big game tomorrow, the team was counting on me, and there was a chance Mr. Barry would show up. But instead of getting a full eight hours, my brain was determined to keep me up all night.

Thinking about Ian and our last conversation.

Why hadn't I said anything? Told him it wasn't over? Said, of course, we were still friends?

I wiped a stray tear from my face.

Because I'd been too chicken. And deep down, I had wanted him to hurt, like he had hurt me.

The thought of letting him hurt me again…

I rolled around and pressed my face against my pillow, letting out a frustrated groan.

Then the perfect solution popped into my head.

A time machine! Duh!

I could just go back in time, not kiss Ian on that

dare. And definitely not accept *his* dare about becoming my fake boyfriend.

We would still be friends…

Where was a time machine when you needed one?

Oh wait, this was reality.

I was stuck with all the choices I'd made, including the one to let him walk away, take all the blame.

Not tell him how I really felt.

I went back to staring at the ceiling, only the street light several feet outside my window casting a small ray of light into my room.

It was two in the morning, and I had to be up in less than five hours…

At some point, I must have fallen asleep because, the next thing I knew, my six-thirty alarm was going off and I just wanted to cry and pretend it was Saturday.

Maybe if it wasn't a big game day, I would have begged my mom to let me stay home, convince her I had a fever or cramps or something.

But missing the semifinals? One of the biggest games of the year?

I sucked it up, unglued my eyelids, and splashed my face with cold water.

Tired eyes stared back at me in the bathroom mirror. I looked like a zombie.

Pulling out my make-up bag, I sighed, knowing I'd need to pile it on thick today to cover the dark circles.

When I got back to my room, I picked up my phone, sure I was running late. But what stood out was a message from Ian.

It said delivered at 3:47am, and I wondered how I had missed it earlier.

Probably because I'd only fully opened my eyes after stumbling to the bathroom.

I read the message.

Ian: Are you awake? Sorry if I'm waking you, but I just have to say this because I can't sleep. Everything we said last time we talked keeps replaying in my head like a bad song, and I hate that it even happened. The truth is I don't want to lose you. As a friend. Or otherwise. Maybe for you it was all fake. Maybe not. I don't know. But being with you, Lena, is the most real thing I've ever done. I'm sorry about everything. I'm sorry I even asked you to do this for me. It messed everything up, and it's my fault. I should have known it was a bad idea, but I think deep down, part of me felt something for you, and I wanted to see what it would be like. To touch you. Hug you, as more than a friend. Maybe kiss you. The more time went by, the more I realized I was falling for you, not trying to get my ex back. This stopped being about her a long time ago. I don't care if you don't feel the same way about us. It doesn't matter. But can we just go back to where we were before? I miss you. I miss sitting with you on the bus to games or sitting together on the bleachers. I hope you'll give our friendship another chance… See you at the game.

He had never sent me a longer message. And not one like this.

I read it one more time, not believing it was real.

Then that sinking feeling in my stomach came back, and I felt like throwing up. I closed my text messages, unable to reply. Not now.

Maybe tonight… Ian wanted to fix this. It

sounded like he had feelings for me too, but maybe I could convince him that being anything more than friends...wasn't a good idea.

I wasn't ready. I didn't want risk our friendship again. I didn't want to let him down before his game. But hopefully, he'd understand. He said so right there that it was okay to just be friends, right?

That's what I would do.

This whole kissing for realsies thing was no joke, and the thought of doing it again scared me more than the possibility of losing the state championship game. Even more than letting my team down.

Nope.

This dare had ruined all kinds of kissing for me, but especially kissing Ian.

No matter how I felt about him.

———

TORI PUT her water bottle down with a slam on the cafeteria table. "ARE YOU CRAZY?"

I failed to meet her eyes, instead focusing on the cheesy nachos in front of me. "Uh..."

This was not the reaction I had been expecting after telling the #BFFs about Ian's 3am message.

Harper bit her lip, looking kind of sheepish. Probably because she agreed with Tori.

Ella put her hand on my arm. "Why haven't you texted him back?"

Rey crossed her arms, no longer interested in

writing whatever she had been writing. "I want to know too."

All of a sudden, I felt like my mom was yelling at me for not taking out the trash like I was supposed to.

Tori still didn't seem happy, except she momentarily channeled her fury toward Rey. "Text him back? She needs to talk to him! Have a conversation." She turned back to me, waiting for a response.

I scoffed, annoyed with myself for not fibbing a little and letting them see I didn't care about Ian as more than a friend. "Gee, thanks, Mom," I teased, just a tad of annoyance slipping through in my voice. "I don't want to, okay? I mean, yes, I'll talk to him. But later, after the game. Or tomorrow. No need to get your pom-poms in a twist."

Harper pushed her tray away, clearly caring more about this situation than the half-eaten slice of pizza on her plate. "That's fine, if all you want to be is friends. But I think we all know that's not true, Lena. P.S. we love you, okay?"

Ella nodded. "We're on your side. Promise. But you're cheating yourself *and* Ian by insisting that you don't like him."

Tori popped a cherry tomato into her mouth. "I sense a little denial too."

Rey held back a smile, and I groaned. "Ughhhh, you guys are the worst," I cried. But I knew they were right. "Just a day or two of denial, that's all I ask." I put my head in my hands. "Why do I let all of you guys' goody goodness rub off on me…"

At least that had them giggling.

I sighed, the sinking feeling in my stomach improving a little. Which probably meant they were right.

My dad's words to me last night came back.

The worst part was that they all made sense. My friends. My dad.

I *was* strong, strong enough to tell Ian the complete truth and not freak out. Not run away or stay silent again.

Just the thought of it made me want to hide, though.

"I'm not like you guys," I said, waving my arms. "I can't just tell a guy how I feel."

Rey sighed. "You're not the only one…"

She used her journal to cover her face up to her eyes, and I gave her a side hug.

"What would I do without you?" I said. "Finally, someone on my side."

Then she lowered her journal. "I still think you should tell Ian how you feel, though."

I took back my hug. "Rey….I thought we were cool," I joked, pretend sad facc on.

She smiled. "I just think there are times in life where you only get one shot, you know? Better to have loved and lost than not have loved at all and all that. Don't you think? I'm still trying to work up the courage myself, but seeing the mighty Lena do it would be a good nudge for me." She winked, still waiting for me to say I would do it.

Tori gave me a look like she knew she was right.

Ella and Harper at least had the decency to look sympathetic.

I sighed, knowing when I had lost a battle. "Fii-ine," I said, drawing out the word for like ten seconds.

Tori leaned in. "You know what you gotta do. Go after him, Lena. Tell him how you feel. For real."

Harper nodded. "He obviously feels the same way, girl."

Ella said, "Yep. I concur."

I doubted that Ian felt the same way after I'd blown off his text message. "Obviously? I don't know about obviously…" But that weird feeling was back.

Tori crossed her arms. "Come on, where's the brave and daring Lena we know? The one who would take on any dare without the blink of an eye?"

"Hello!" I cried. "I'm in this situation thanks to a dare. Besides, there are real feelings involved now, okay?? Kissing for fun was easy. This is not."

That had all of them laughing again and Rey wrapping her arm around me again but also laughing.

Part of me wanted to cry. Part of me wanted to just run away and maybe change schools.

But I knew my friends were right. I had to tell Ian my truth.

So many chances to tell him how I really felt about him, and I hadn't had the courage to do it. Well, it was time to muster up some.

In truth or dare, I had always gone with dare. Dare was easy. Fun. Crazy.

Truth was hard. Letting someone in? Hard. Telling someone you like like them? Scary.

Meeting Ian's eyes and telling him it had been real for me too? Just thinking about it made me want to panic.

I looked at the #BFFs. "What if it doesn't work out? What if he says—"

Ella took my hand. "Whatever happens, you'll be okay."

Harper said, "We're with you either way."

Rey opened up her journal again. "You won't know until you try, Lena."

Tori came around and gave me a quick hug from behind. "You got this," she said softly.

I swallowed the lump in my throat, pushing back tears and determined to make a joke. "Gosh, Tori. You sure know how to dish out the tough love, huh?"

TWENTY-FIVE

Lena: Are you guys sure I shouldn't wait to tell him until AFTER the game? What if we have another fight and we lose because of it?

I hid in one of the bathroom stalls in the locker room and waited for a response from the #BFFs. Katie and the rest of the girls were already busy warming up out on the soccer field.

I'd assured them I'd be right out, and they'd asked me if I was okay, if I needed some Advil or something. I'd finally convinced them to leave. After promising that there wouldn't be a repeat of that one game.

We still had some time before the game, and I could have just saved my talk with Ian for tonight.

But the #BFFs were pushing me to talk to him now.

And another, more important reason I needed to stop being so chicken and confront him?

He hadn't been doing so well.

I knew for a fact he'd been tardy this morning, missed most of first period. Looked like a zombie. He hadn't even shown up for lunch, and the varsity boys' team was worried about him.

And understandably so. One of the big reasons they had made it to the state championship game tonight was thanks to Ian. He'd easily blocked a dozen or more goals this season, and there was no way they would win tonight if he was not on top of his game.

Chris had already pleaded with me before fourth period, to talk to Ian, maybe give him a little encouragement. Then he'd winked, and I had rolled my eyes and walked off.

But I knew they were all right. I couldn't let Ian go on and cost the team a big victory like this because he didn't know the truth. Because I was too scared to tell him the truth.

So despite the nudges and pushes from Tori, Ella, Harper, and Rey, what really convinced me to step out of the locker room and head to where I knew Ian would be hanging out before the game was that. Ian.

I knew how much winning this game would mean to him, and I didn't want him to miss out on it due to what was happening between us.

The truth was I liked him more than ever, and if it meant putting myself out there and possibly getting rejected because I'd done this too late, then so be it.

I saw his lone figure at the very top of the bleachers on the other side of the field where the varsity girls were practicing. Katie waved to me, but I kept walking toward Ian, my hands shoved inside the front pocket of my hoodie.

One by one, I climbed the steps of the metal bleachers to the top. Ian sat on the second to top row, leaning back and resting his feet on the row below him.

He had his warm-ups on, which meant he was in his sweats and hoodie. The air was chilly, but the sun was shining, and I took that as a good sign for what I was about to do.

Either the weird turn our friendship had taken the last several weeks would finally be fixed, one way or another.

Or this might be the end of everything.

The closer I got to the top of the bleachers, the more my heart pounded, the more my legs felt like bags of sand, and I felt like throwing up.

But I kept climbing anyway, my eyes fixed on Ian.

He must have been listening to his playlist on high volume because he didn't hear me come up. He'd been staring off in the other direction, at the sky. When I was just a few feet away, he finally snapped his head in my direction.

Usually, his eyes lit up when he saw me and he smiled, just effortlessly.

Today, he didn't. He sat up, pulled out his earbuds, and waited for me to say something. His eyes questioned why I was there, his mouth parted slightly, and I ached for his grin.

"Hey," I said, sitting down next to him. He scooted away a little, giving me room, I was sure, but it felt more like there was a wall between us, and I couldn't get past it.

I was ready to tear it down, no matter how scary it would be.

He glanced at me than stared down at his phone. "Hey," he said quietly.

"Sorry if I…" my voice trailed off. I coughed, trying to get my jumbled thoughts together.

His eyes met mine. "It's okay."

I exhaled, wondering how to start.

We stared at the girls and guys down below. Passing, shooting, sitting on the grass. Laughing and playing.

Usually, this was our spot before a home game. Listen to music together. Eventually climb down and join the others. Stretch, practice a little as the stands began to fill up.

Today, it felt like I was sitting with a stranger.

I opened my mouth to finally say something because sooner or later Coach was going to make us climb down and warm up. "Ian, I—"

"Lena—" he began at the same time.

We turned to face each other. My eyes automatically went to his mouth, and I remembered what it felt like to get lost in a kiss with him.

Why did it feel like so long ago?

He opened his mouth to talk again, but I raised my hand and pressed a finger against his lips. "Me first."

I took my hand back, and he stayed silent. Meanwhile, inside my chest, my heart raced.

I willed myself to take a deep breath and not rush what I wanted to say. "Ian, I, uh…" I swallowed the rising nausea in my throat and made myself look him in the eyes. "I need you to know that what we had… was real for me too. I just…was too much of a chicken to say it before. I let you walk away thinking I didn't see you as more than a friend, and I should have said something." I paused for half a second. "I know—maybe you just want to stay friends and put all of this behind us, but I want you—"

Ian stopped me, his hand squeezing mine. "Lena, you don't even know how long I've been in love with you," Ian said. Then something weird happened. He began laughing, and I stared at him like a doofus trying to comprehend what he had just said.

"What?" I asked, incredulous.

But I was so happy his smile was back, and the more I understood what he had just said, the bigger my smile grew too.

Was this really happening? Or was I dreaming?

This had to be a dream.

He glanced down then back at me. "I just was always so afraid to tell you. I mean…I thought it would freak you out and you'd stop talking to me or something. So I kind of gave up on you, tried to stop seeing you that way. I mean, why would you ever see me as more than just a friend?" His face fell a little. "Then I started going out with Bethany."

Ian went on, shaking his head. "What happened with Bethany at Homecoming? It was stupid. I only danced with her because she insisted and she said her date ditched her. I felt bad for her. Then she kissed me out of nowhere. But I was looking for you, Lena. *You're* the one I wanted to dance with. I wanted us to dance all night."

"Really?" I said, sure I had the most idiotic grin on my face. "Why didn't you ever say anything about how you felt…"

He came in closer, his hand still on mine. "I could tell you didn't feel the same way."

I looked away, knowing he was right. I hadn't thought of him like that until a few weeks into the dare.

He went on. "I just didn't dare tell you and mess up what we had. You're not like other girls," he said. "I didn't want to be another guy you kissed for fun."

I looked at him again, still attempting to process what he was saying

He shrugged. "Before…just wasn't the right time. Then we did the dare, and I realized I still felt the same way about you. It wasn't just a dare anymore, you know?"

I nodded. "Yeah, I just…couldn't believe it. And I didn't want to mess this up either. The thought of us not being friends anymore…"

"I was okay with us not being friends," Ian said. That made me look up. "I wanted to be more."

Then he leaned in until his mouth was on mine. My eyes closed on their own, and I let everything else disappear. All I wanted to think about was Ian and the way his lips moved against mine. My hands went around his neck, pulling him in closer, while his arms settled around my waist.

What could have been either five seconds or five minutes later, he pulled away slightly. "You don't know how long I've been wanting to do that," he confessed.

Then I laughed and pulled him in close for a hug. "I missed you," I whispered.

He hugged me back, and I sighed and closed my eyes, letting my head rest on his shoulder. "I missed you too."

Then he kissed my forehead, and I wished we could stay like that forever.

However, the sounds of cheers and whoops from down below had us pulling apart.

We turned to the soccer field to find both the boys' and girls' varsity soccer teams screaming and jumping up and down not too far away.

Chris bellowed, "It was about time you two kissed and made up!"

I turned to Ian, and we laughed.

From across the field, Coach came out of the boys' locker room, where his office was, and blew his whistle. "You two lovebirds get down here and start warming up!"

When we stepped onto the grass, Chris came up to me and gave us a hug. Katie and the girls hugged me too.

Chris said, "Finally! We have a real chance of winning this thing now."

TWENTY-SIX

The girls played first.

Maybe because I had been practicing my butt off or maybe because I was still kind of high from the adrenaline of kissing Ian earlier, but I played like never before, making an impossible pass to Katie who then made a goal. All during the first ten minutes of the game.

It was a tough team, though, and they didn't let us make another easy goal. Almost like we had awoken a hibernating, very aggressive bear. But we wanted this too. And we weren't going to let them score if we could help it.

Toward the end of the second half, their best forward kicked the ball hard toward the right lower corner. It was a good shot, one our goalie just couldn't stop. Just like that, we were suddenly tied. Which meant victory could easily go either way.

We had to score another goal, or we wouldn't walk away with a state championship trophy.

The more the game went on and the sun went down, the more the bleachers filled up with students, parents, and teachers who'd shown up to support the school.

The screams of my friends reached me. Tori, Ella, Harper, and Rey stood up and cheered the whole time, sign and all. Tori had even brought her pompoms for good measure.

With just fifteen minutes left in the game, I blew them a kiss.

From the bleachers, Mr. Barry also watched. Thinking about him too much made me nervous. Sometimes he jotted notes; other times, he just crossed his arms and watched. I reminded myself to forget about him and focus on the ball, on the opposing players around me.

Soccer was all about finding the right opportunity. I just had to find mine.

There.

A girl from the other team messed up a pass, kicking it too far my way.

I reached it before her teammate. Dribbled it the opposite direction toward the goal, keeping an eye out for defenders.

Barely dodged one. Almost tripped. Heard Katie's scream of "Open!" as she ran toward the goal several feet away.

A couple of defenders ran toward me, and I kicked the ball across to Katie. My lungs screamed for me to slow down and breathe, but I pushed myself to run faster and help Katie out. She maneuvered the ball this way and that, keeping it out of reach of the other team, but she couldn't keep that up for much longer. She searched for someone to pass to.

"Katie!" I screamed. In the background, I was pretty sure everyone in the bleachers was screaming their heads off, but the sounds seemed far away. Even though I was sprinting like my life depended on it, everything happened in slow motion. My heart pounded in my ears, the rest of the world silent.

The ball at her feet, Katie eyed me for the tiniest fraction of a second. I knew what that meant. I glanced around, gauging how much room I had.

A second later, she faked one way then kicked the ball long and hard toward me. With defenders surrounding me, I knew I wouldn't have long to take a shot.

It would be now or never because the game was almost over. Our team would not get another chance like this to shoot.

Across the field, Perry screamed at me for a pass, getting the other team's attention long enough for me to get control of the ball and turn it around.

I kept my arms out, giving myself space. I could not lose the ball now.

I dribbled fast toward the goal, a defender behind me, just a couple away. She tried to kick the ball away. Just a touch would send the ball flying and ruin my chance at the goal.

Ahead of me, the goalie got in position, her stance low, her arms out. Ready to jump and block the ball.

This was it. The opposing player pushed against

me, but I held my body firm. Kept running. Eyed the ball. Got it in position and…kicked it with everything I had, where it needed to go clear in my mind.

It flew, flew, flew…

The goalie jumped, reached…

I jogged to a stop…

Watched it go in right at the corner of the net!

Screams erupted from the stands, and I jumped up and down. Katie ran over and hugged me. We jumped together with the rest of the team, screaming because we had done it.

The referee blew the whistle, signaling for a new kickoff.

Coach yelled at us from the sidelines, "Two minutes left!"

The stands chanted at our defense, and slowly, the seconds counted down.

The other team had the ball now, dodged this way and that. Then, one of their forwards took a long shot at our goal. Missed the net completely.

Then the buzzer went off, and the crowd began screaming and jumping up and down. Adrenaline coursed through me. We had done it.

I ran toward the rest of the team and landed the perfect roundoff. We jumped and screamed together.

Katie squeezed me. "I knew we could do it!"

We enveloped our goalie, who'd easily blocked a handful of shots to our goal. "You were amazing," I told her.

The entire team found Coach just off the field and in front of the stands. Mr. Green, acting as announcer tonight, held up our trophy, a gleaming gold soccer ball at the top of a pedestal, in his hand. He raised a microphone to his face with the other. Over the speakers, we heard the words I'd been waiting for all season: "Ladies and gentleman, I present to you the varsity girls soccer state champions... the Lady Eagles!"

He handed us the trophy, and Katie and I took it, holding it up for the world to see. Pretty sure there was a solid minute of screaming and jumping before we took the trophy to our Coach.

More screaming and clapping.

As the other team left the field, heads down, the boys came down to celebrate along with us.

I had to find Ian.

Spotting him just a few feet away, I ran to him and wrapped my arms around his neck.

He whispered in my ear, "You were incredible."

I looked at him. "Thanks. And you're up next."

He already looked nervous.

I took his hands. "You've got this." Then I got on my tip toes and reached up for him, closing my eyes as my lips pressed against his.

A familiar grunt brought me back down to Earth, and Ian's gaze settled on someone behind us.

My dad, who could hardly meet my eyes. Much less Ian's.

Ian shook his hand, muttered something about warming up with the rest of the team, and disappeared.

My dad put his arm around me, and we walked

off the field with the rest of the girls' team. Most of them headed to the stands to cheer on the boys. We had posters and chants ready, but I could tell my dad wanted to say something. On the sidelines, he stood in front of me, nodding slightly. "You did very good out there, *mija*," he said quietly. "Very good."

I gave him a hug, and it hit me that this would be our last major game of the season. We'd have an away tournament later on, but this was it. There wouldn't be another season of soccer in high school. And my dad wouldn't take on the same role of coaching me like before, not if I was away at college. I squeezed him harder. "Thanks, Dad. For everything."

We pulled away, and all he did was nod again, hardly making eye contact, but it was more than enough for me.

Coach walked over then, Mr. Barry right behind him. He shook my dad's hand then mine. "Congratulations, Ms. Martinez," he said. "I definitely look forward to talking to you soon about your options for next year. I know you still have a few months left in your senior year, but you'll definitely have some important decisions ahead of you."

I beamed. "Thank you. I can't wait."

The three of them continued talking, and I exhaled, my hand to my chest. So my hard work had paid off after all.

Not too far away, the #BFFs waved to me, huddled together near the bleachers.

I ran over and screamed one more time for good measure.

After we exchanged hugs, Ella took my hands. "Lena, you were awesome out there!"

Tori nodded. "And that roundoff at the end? Not bad." We laughed.

Rey looked a little confused. "This was definitely not like basketball," she said.

Harper put her arm around her. "I didn't understand what was going on half the time, but when you made that goal at the end, wow. You're crazy talented, you know that?"

I glanced at Tori. She knew. "A little bit of talent. A lot of hard work, but thank you." I bowed. "So you guys want to stay for the guy's game? I can explain it to you, and we're all going out to eat after—"

Ella said, "We're in!"

I held up my finger. "Just one more thing. I'll catch up to you guys on the bleachers."

I turned and found Ian, already warming up at the goal. I ran toward him. He met me halfway. "What is it?" he asked.

I shrugged. "I just needed to wish you good luck and do this," I said, practically jumping into this arms. He caught me, his arms around my waist, and I put my hands around his face, bringing him close.

The air was chilly, but being this close to Ian? It lit a fire inside me.

My mouth moved against his, letting him know just how much he meant to me.

We pulled apart, and he stared down at me. "Whoa," he said.

I giggled. "Tell me about it."

Then he turned around and jogged back to his post, glancing back at me one more time with those beautiful baby blue eyes and dazzling smile. I was pretty sure I was smiling like an idiot, biting my lip and savoring the kiss from just seconds ago.

But I didn't care.

Kissing for funsies couldn't compare to this.

Kissing someone for real.

Kissing someone who'd been my friend for ages and now meant so much more.

As I turned and headed for the bleachers, I couldn't help but think that senior year couldn't get better than this.

EPILOGUE

Thanks to Ian's ninja goalkeeping skills—and our non-stop cheerleading of the crowd—, the boys won 3-1, winning a state title along with us. After it was all over, we found ourselves at the Shake Shack.

The #BFFs along with Jesse, Emerson, and Noah joined us along with several other people from school.

The sole cook in the kitchen looked at the collective order of burgers and fries, and we thought he might pass out. But, holding his spatula steady, he got to work.

Meanwhile, the waitress appeased us with fries.

Ian sat next to me, his arm around me like that night so long ago.

In reality, it had been only about a month ago.

Maybe what made it feel so far away was that now we were in a completely different place.

No longer on a dare, for one.

Just a regular relationship, which it turned out, was the best kind.

Before, I might have thought of that as boring or not for me.

But it was way more fun and meant so much more than any other experience I'd had with a guy.

Being with Ian?

It felt right and completely natural.

From the corner of my eye, Tori caught my attention. She aimed her phone at us. "Don't mind me," she said. "You two are so cute. I had to take a picture."

"In that case," I said, turning to Ian and kissing him on the cheek.

He blushed a little, and Tori laughed, snapping another picture.

She handed me her phone. "We're totally getting prints of these."

I showed Ian the picture, his expression serious the longer he stared at us.

I smiled. "Are you okay?"

He bit his lip and looked at me with that same look. "Yeah, I just…feel like the luckiest guy in the world right now," he said quietly, his eyes locked on mine.

I just wanted to wrap my arms around him again, but Harper's voice made me turn back to the others. "We should totally do a group picture!"

I flagged down Katie and handed her my phone while the rest of us squeezed into the booth or kneeled on the seat of the booth behind ours. Putting my arm around Ian, I smiled for the picture.

Ella told Rey, "Get in here," and Katie counted down and took the picture.

She gave me my phone back, and I pulled up the photo, falling in love with it immediately.

"You have to send that to everyone," Ella said.

In the first row sat Ian, myself, Tori, and Noah. Behind us, stood Rey, Harper, Emerson, Ella, and Jesse. All of us grinning and with our arms around each other.

I pulled up Instagram. "I'm so posting this. I'll tag you guys."

Rey looked at the picture as I added the perfect filter. "Maybe Cupid will finally remember to find someone for me," she teased.

I nudged her playfully with my hip. "I thought you already liked what's his name?" I asked.

Her face turned pink. "That's just a silly crush," she replied, glancing away.

"I don't know," I said. "In the time we've known each other, that's the one guy you've always had a thing for. Besides, you said that if I told Ian how I felt, that it would give you the courage to do the same with your crush."

I looked at her expectantly, and she began backing away slowly like she might make a run for it. "I—I do not remember saying that…"

"Oh, I do," I said, hitting post on my picture, sticking my phone in my back pocket, and taking a step toward her. "Tori, I have something to ask you!" I teased.

Panic filled her face. "Lena, no!" she whisper shouted.

I put my hands on my hips.

Her shoulders slumped, and we took a seat again. "I promise I'll think about it, okay?"

I nudged her again. "Okay," I said. "But don't wait forever, okay? Don't let fear hold you back. You never know what could happen."

I turned to Ian, who was busy chatting with Noah, Jesse, and Emerson. It made me happy to see Ian hanging out with them, talking like they'd been friends forever.

Rey's thoughts interrupted my own. "It's weird to even think about having a boyfriend. It just doesn't feel like it could ever happen for me, you know?"

I gave her a side hug. "Rey, of course, it'll happen for you. And when you least expect it."

She sighed. "I'm not sure it'll be that easy…"

Tori, Harper, and Ella joined us in our booth while the guys continued chatting at the next table.

Ella sighed. "Can you guys believe how fast senior year is flying by? I just want time to stop."

Harper leaned her head on Ella's shoulder. "Me too. I'm going to miss this."

Rey frowned. "I can't even think about it. It makes me too sad."

Tori took her hand. "I know, but it's also exciting, don't you think? We'll be adulting and everything."

I laughed. "Okay, don't say adulting."

We giggled.

YESENIA VARGAS

Harper glanced at Emerson, and Tori did the same. "There's so much to figure out," she said.

"So we'll figure it out," I said. "And no matter what, I know we'll stick together. We'll always stay friends." I put my hand in the middle of the table. Then Ella put hers on top. Then Tori. Harper. And finally, Rey. "Here's to an amazing rest of senior year." I put my other hand on top. "Not to mention graduating together. And remaining best friends."

Tori smiled. "I completely agree."

Ella said, "A year from now. Five years from now…"

Harper said, "Always."

Rey finally gave us a smile. "Forever."

———

FIVE FRIENDS. Five Christmas wishes. Five chances for things to go horribly wrong.

Check out the #BFFs' Christmas adventure, #AllIWant-ForChristmas, now: https://www.amazon.-com/gp/product/B07KTKH23K/

AUTHOR'S NOTE

Hey :)
        You made it! <3

I have so many feels about this story. Right from the start, **Lena and her voice just grabbed me.** Her story was a LOT of fun to write! Haha.

From the beginning, **I knew that she was the extrovert of the group, the loud and crazy one.** Kind of like Bridget from the Sisterhood of the Travelings Pants, and they also happen to share a love for soccer.

In fact, that was definitely **one of my favorite things about this story: channeling my own love for soccer.**

Fun fact: I played for many years, starting in high school, but the position I ended up in (and loving) was actually goalkeeper (same as Ian).

#TheBoyfriendDare had its share of ups and downs, though.

The book felt like it took me FOREVER to write. I wasn't too far in when several things happened, and **the story came to a halt** for well over a month. Almost two.

- **my kids and I got a horrible virus** one right after another; I'm talking vomit non-stop…

- **that next week, I traveled to Las Vegas** for an epic writing conference; I also happened to get strep the day I had to leave!

- I got back, ready to dive back into writing then… **I got a call one night from my older sister Ana that she had gone into labor. Ah!** I grabbed my stuff and was out the door in about 5 minutes. Spent several days with her and the baby as they got adjusted.

- **we hosted Thanksgiving**; tons of family time; I took a few days off afterward to just REST after everything.

- By this time, I had been away from the story for such a long time that **I felt completely lost. Unable to write, uninspired, full of self-doubt.**

Slowly but surely, though—and after a wrong turn or two—**I found Lena's voice again :)**

I can't believe how much happened during the writing of it, but it's **just another reason her story is extra special for me.**

Another part that meant a lot to me was **Lena's relationship with her dad. I would say that my dad is very similar in that he also very rarely**

shares his emotions. Other than that, he tends to be more like Lena: loud, extroverted, makes people laugh. But it was cool taking a small part of my own dad and using that as inspiration for Lena's dad.

Right now, **I'm more than halfway done with Rey's story and the last book in the series! I**'ll admit there's some pressure that comes with getting this book right and making sure it ties up the story nicely, but I'm hoping it'll work out in the end!

If you want to know when Rey's book is available, make sure you sign up for my newsletter and become a VIP reader :)

In the meantime, I'd love to hear what you thought of #TheBoyfriendDare and which #BFF is your favorite.

Email me your thoughts and questions at hello@yeseniavargas.com. You can count on me to reply!

Book 5 Coming Soon!

I'm already hard at work on **Rey's story!** Are you as excited about that as I am? You should be :)

It'll be available in spring 2019.

To be the first to know when it releases, make sure you become a VIP reader ASAP!

For now, make sure you check out the bonus Christmas novella in the #BestFriends-Forever series!

Five friends. Five Christmas wishes. Five chances for things to go horribly wrong.

Become a VIP Reader & Download Your Bonus Content!

Become a VIP Reader today and get access to all of your **exclusive bonus content**, including:

- the short story of how Baller929 and TheRealCinderella met (from Baller929's point of view!)
- exclusive sneak peeks of the next book in the series!
- plus fun updates & pictures of me and my kids you won't find anywhere else

My youngest daughter, Celeste, and me :)

You will be nearly as cool as Celeste once you sign up ;)

What are you waiting for? Become a VIP reader and download your bonus content today!

I'll send more pictures of my kids :) Promise.

Sign up right now at: www.yeseniavargas.-com/bff4

Don't Forget to Leave a Review!

If you enjoyed this book and would like to see more books from me, make sure to write a review **(just a couple sentences is okay)!**

Reviews help other readers find my books, so **thank you in advance!**

Once again, thank you for reading #TheBoyfriendDare!

I'll see you in the next book :)

YESENIA

ACKNOWLEDGMENTS

Thank you once again to all of these amazing people:

My husband, who is a huge help and one of my biggest supporters.

My two amazing little girls, whose kisses and hugs sustained me these past several months. They more than made up for the constant interruptions :)

My best friend and biggest fan, Zendy <3 Your never-ending support and encouragement means the world to me.

My YA Chicks group of friends, including Sally, Cindy, and Kelsie. Thank you for all the feedback, support, and encouragement! And making Thursday nights fun :) Can't wait to hang out with you guys in person again!

My Thursday Night Inferno accountability group. Your friendship, support, and encouragement means more than you know.

My cover designer, Jenny, who nailed this cover. Thank you so much for being a part of my team.

My VIP Readers and Awesome Review Team. Thank you so much for being patient, reading the story, and helping me spread the word about #TheBoyfriendDare. You guys are my favorite :)

ABOUT THE AUTHOR

Yesenia Vargas is the author of several young adult romance books. Her love for writing stories was born from her love of reading and books. She has her third grade teacher to thank for that.

In addition to writing and reading, she spends her time hanging out with her family, working out, and binge-watching Netflix. In 2013, she graduated from the University of Georgia, the first in her family to go to college.

Yesenia lives in Georgia with her husband and two precious little girls. She also blogs at writermom.net

Check out what she's up to at yeseniavargas.com.

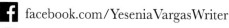

facebook.com/YeseniaVargasWriter

instagram.com/thisiswritermom

ALSO BY YESENIA VARGAS

#BestFriendsForever Series

#TheRealCinderella

#LoveToHateThatBoy

#GoodGirlBadBoy

#TheBoyfriendDare

#AllIWantForChristmas

Find all the download links as well as a complete list of my most recent books at yeseniavargas.com/books/.

54363415R00136

Made in the USA
San Bernardino,
CA